DREAM STORM

Look for other REMNANTS™
titles by K.A. Applegate:

Also by K.A. Applegate:
ANIMORPHS®

REMNANTS™

DREAM STORM

K.A. APPLEGATE

AN
APPLE
PAPERBACK

SCHOLASTIC INC.
New York Toronto London Auckland Sydney
Mexico City New Delhi Hong Kong Buenos Aires

ISBN 0-590-88495-6

12 11 10 9 8 7 6 5 4 3 2 1   3 4 5 6 7 8/0

Printed in the U.S.A.   40
First printing, March 2003

For Michael and Jake

DREAM STORM

CHAPTER ONE

"LIKE LETTING GO OF A LIFELINE."

Mo'Steel wasn't going to cry. True, they were now stranded on the lifeless Earth. Pretty much dead men walking. But he'd just have to suck it up and go on. No use bunnying out.

"Mom, Mom, it's gonna be okay," he said soothingly.

Olga was standing next to him, biting her bottom lip, eyes filled with tears. Her eyes were locked on the sooty sky, even though Mother was no longer visible.

Mother was a strange, massive ship. A ship with a consciousness — or at least a ship built around a computer so advanced she could experience emotion. Like anger. And loneliness.

Mother had been lonely. Lonely ever since the beings that had created her had fallen into conflict and disseminated themselves, leaving her drifting through space. So when she spotted the Remnants' space shuttle, she eagerly snatched it out of the sky and woke them up from five-hundred-years' worth of hibernation to keep her company.

Most of the time since then they'd been at her mercy. Action figures in a game they were forced to play to amuse her.

A deadly game.

Among the Remnants only one of them had proven to be Mother's match. Billy. She came to care for him, and he'd used his influence over her to help the Remnants gain some control of the massive ship. Eventually, they managed to turn her back toward the ruined Earth.

Ruined because an asteroid the size of New Jersey had whacked the planet silly. They called the asteroid the Rock, and it was the reason they'd left Earth in the first place.

Mo'Steel, Jobs, and the others had dealt with death and hunger and war and sabotage and some very unpleasant green worms to make it back home.

Then, when things couldn't possibly get worse, things got worse. They'd learned Earth was seemingly unable to support life: no food, no water. And they were abandoned on the broken planet by Yago, a spoiled brat who was convinced he was superior and who wanted control of the ship for his own purposes. The other Remnants assumed he had some help from the Troika — Amelia, Duncan, and Charlie — another faction with their own mysterious agenda. Tate was up there, too. She'd still been on the ship when Yago took off.

"Mom?" Mo'Steel said. "Come on, don't cry."

"I — I'm fine," Olga said haltingly. She dragged her eyes slowly away from the sky and met Mo'-Steel's gaze. "It's just — letting go of the ship is like letting go of a lifeline."

"We're *not* going to die," Mo'Steel said defiantly.

But so many were gone already. There were only eleven Remnants now — not counting Yago and the other people still on the ship.

Mo'Steel ran his gaze over his companions, trying to gauge how they were holding up. Not too well, it seemed.

Depressing. But justified.

Those kids in *Lord of the Flies* were angels compared to a few people in this group.

2Face included.

At the moment, she was sitting cross-legged in the ash next to Billy. She looked small, scared, and lonely with her dark hair hiding her scarred face, murmuring softly, trying desperately to wake Billy up. She *looked* defenseless, but Mo'Steel knew better. 2Face had proven again and again that her own survival was her main interest.

And then there was Violet.

Something in her expression concerned Mo'Steel. She was standing with her hands on her hips, suspiciously watching the four Blue Meanies that had been abandoned on Earth with them.

The Meanies. They were the same size and build as ponies. They wore midnight-blue armorlike suits fitted with rockets and weapons. The Meanies looked lost, ridiculously out of place huddled together near a hunk of concrete. They communicated by a form of sign language, waving the tentacles bracketing their faces — and judging by the speed of the waving, it looked as if they were having a pretty massive argument.

Maybe Violet was right to watch them so carefully. The Meanies could be very dangerous and they weren't especially fond of humans. The two groups had fought bitterly for control of Mother. *We both lost,* Mo'Steel thought. This was just another dark plot twist in a long, sad story.

D-Caf and Roger Dodger — Mo'Steel thought they were strapping it up okay. They were a few steps away from Violet, watching her protectively.

Jobs. Jobs was a rock, as usual. Mo'Steel's best

friend had one arm slung over his little brother's shoulders. Mo'Steel could hardly see the kid, Edward. His skin had turned ash-colored like his surroundings. Edward — like so many of them — had experienced mutation. Now he was a human chameleon.

And then there was Noyze. She was standing alone, her eyes wide and wild looking.

"Yo, Noyze!" Mo'Steel called. "Over here."

Noyze looked at him, smiled weakly, and headed his way. Mo'Steel reminded himself to be strong for his favorite fem, even if the situation did look beyond bleak.

The situation — and the scenery. No doubt it was hard to be gung-ho in all this unrelenting gray. Mo'Steel guessed that billions of pounds of ash had rained down and filled in the rubble of what had once been Tokyo. The wind drove the ash up into the air where it made Mo'Steel's eyes and skin itch and clogged his nose with an ashy crust.

Here and there some random thing poked out of the ash: a stretch of broken stairs reaching up into the sky, a hunk of concrete with exposed rebar. The tallest thing near them was a circular brick chimney maybe two stories tall.

"Ouch," Noyze mumbled, stumbling.

"Careful!" Olga called to her.

Walking across the ash landscape was dicey. The ash hid the occasional tiny shard of — whatever. The rubble beneath their feet was constantly settling, shifting, collapsing. A few times they'd seen a flaming pillar of gas appear without warning. One of these gas eruptions had swallowed Burroway. True, Burroway wasn't the nicest person, but thinking about him reminded Mo'Steel of yet another way they could be hurt or killed.

"We can't stay here," Olga said.

"No," Mo'Steel agreed, but he couldn't imagine where else they could go. "Maybe Jobs or Billy —"

"Get down!" someone yelled.

Mo'Steel felt a strange breeze and realized a boomerang had just passed inches from his nose. He tackled his mom, knocking her sideways and sending a plume of ash into the air.

"Riders?" Olga grunted.

"Probably," Mo'Steel said, cursing under his breath. Could this day be any worse?

The Riders were a dangerous, brutal race of aliens that resembled overgrown, two-headed roaches. One head was little more than a mouth stuck on a neck. The other, main head, was dominated by two large, glittery-gold, compound eyes. They rode hoverboards and carried primitive but deadly weapons.

Mo'Steel twisted around on his belly, trying to figure out what was going on.

Anamull.

Anamull was almost hidden by the half-buried remains of a car. He came out of hiding long enough to reach up and snag the boomerang. He squinted one eye, aimed, and let the sharp weapon fly again.

"Noyze!" Mo'Steel yelled.

The others were running for cover, stumbling on the uneven ground. But Noyze could only limp along, her right leg stiff with bandages. A beam from the ruined city had fallen on her the day before.

Now Noyze was caught in the sudden cross fire. The Riders were counterattacking. One of the Blue Meanies took off. Another let loose a stream of fléchettes. They pinged off the brick chimney.

"Noyze — look out!" Olga yelled.

Noyze, confused, froze in her tracks, unsure of which way to go. A boomerang passed a few feet from her head.

Ignoring the bullets and boomerangs and fléchette fire flying over his head, Mo'Steel ran toward Noyze and grabbed her out of the way. They both lost their footing and Mo'Steel felt a sharp pain as a shard of something slammed into his elbow.

"Ow — my leg," Noyze muttered.

"Sorry, I didn't mean for us to fall."

Noyze gave him a weary smile. "I prefer people to save my life with a little more *refinement*."

"I'll try to remember that next time."

Olga began shouting at Anamull and Roger Dodger cried out. Then — silence.

Mo'Steel released Noyze and cautiously raised his head. Anamull was striding toward them. "It's over!" he yelled.

"Great," Noyze grumbled. She pointed off toward the gray horizon. Two Meanies were down. Mo'Steel didn't see the Riders or the other Meanies anywhere. He hoped they weren't lying in ambush somewhere.

"Where'd the other two Meanies go?" Violet called. "And the Riders?"

"Ran off," Anamull said with a nasty laugh. "I guess they were too scared to stay and fight."

Mo'Steel rose shakily to his feet. Noyze started to get up, too. Mo'Steel pointed to her leg and said, "Rest."

Noyze looked down, surprised. "Oh, I'm bleeding."

"Mom!" Mo'Steel called. "Can you come check out Noyze's leg? She's bleeding again."

"Really smart!" Olga hollered angrily at Anamull. "We're in enough trouble as it is. What's the big idea starting a fight?"

Anamull didn't lose his fierce, proud look. "We're gonna need them," he said, jutting his chin toward the fallen Meanies. "For food."

Jobs and Edward ran to Roger Dodger's side. Violet was pressing a piece of fabric — someone's sock, it looked like — to his head to stop the bleeding.

Roger Dodger looked at Jobs with wide, frightened eyes. He was hiccup-breathing, trying hard not to cry. Jobs was reminded that the kid was only ten years old.

"You're going to be okay," Jobs told Roger Dodger. He looked at Violet.

"He's going to be fine," Violet said firmly. "Head wounds always bleed a lot."

Olga appeared at Jobs's side. "Let me see."

Jobs scooted back to make room for Olga. "Is Noyze okay?"

"Fine," Olga said. "A nasty scrape, nothing more."

Jobs took a step back and fought to slow his breathing. He felt dizzy, breathless. *The low oxygen atmosphere must be affecting me,* he thought. The reality of their situation was beginning to sink in and he felt a depression deep in his bones.

Yago had tricked them. How could they survive? Or, more to the point, could they survive at all?

Eleven humans.

A hostile environment.

Four warlike aliens, hiding out somewhere.

And what did they have?

Easy enough for Jobs to make a list. He'd outfitted them — planning for brief scouting trips, not for long-term survival on the planet. Their stuff was more than inadequate, it was a joke.

They each had half a liter of water and a weapon, a couple dozen crackers, eleven lead-lined bags, eleven pairs of gloves, eleven flashlights, eleven oxygen masks, thirty-three liters of oxygen, some shovels and spades, exactly fifty-six feet of rope, the clothes on their backs, the dead Meanies and — Billy. If Billy could communicate with Mother, he could bring her back and save their skins.

The way Jobs saw it, Billy was their only hope for survival.

Once again.

(CHAPTER TWO)

"PLEASE WAKE UP."

"Billy, please, please wake up," 2Face pleaded. Billy lay stretched out motionless beside her. She only knew he was alive because of the faint rise and fall of his chest.

"Billy, please," 2Face said, repulsed by her own voice, by her own stupidity. She felt the others glancing at her and Billy, then shifting their attention elsewhere.

She felt their scorn. They'd trusted her and she'd made a huge mistake: She'd underestimated Yago.

Yago and 2Face had been playing a deadly game. A game of survival they'd started more than five hundred years and many, many moves ago. Getting them to the planet's surface and abandoning them there had been Yago's final move.

Checkmate.

2Face had lost. And now she was going to die here. They all were. Die of exposure and starvation and thirst.

But not just yet.

They still had one more slim chance.

Billy.

Billy had a connection, some sort of human—computer friendship with Mother, the super-advanced brains of the ship.

2Face didn't pretend to understand how the connection worked. Before they'd been abandoned on this wreck of Earth, she'd thought Billy couldn't be disconnected from the ship. That there was nothing to be severed.

But she'd been very, very wrong.

How had Yago done it anyway? Had he gotten the Troika — Amelia, Duncan, and Charlie — to help him control the ship? Amelia and the others claimed to be evolving, turning into some sort of super-beings. Did that mean they'd learned how to fly the ship? And if they had, did that mean Billy couldn't control Mother any longer?

No, 2Face told herself again, biting down on her lip. Billy *can* control Mother. He had to.

"Please, Billy," 2Face said again. "Please wake up."

Nothing.

2Face sat back on her heels. She looked at Billy's still form and felt the anger boiling up from her stomach.

Why hadn't Billy told her coming down to the surface was too dangerous? He must have known. He must have known his connection with Mother was vulnerable. He *should* have warned them.

2Face leaned over, grabbed Billy's shoulders, and began to shake him. "Wake up! Wake up now!"

Hands now on her shoulders. Many pairs, pulling her away from Billy.

"Whoa, that's enough!" Mo'Steel said angrily.

"She's hysterical." Noyze.

2Face thrashed, kicking her feet as the others hauled her backward. Something under the ash grabbed hold of her right shoe and pulled it free of her foot. "Let me go. He has to wake up!"

They let her go about fifty yards from Billy. "Let me deal with him my way," 2Face said, scrambling to her feet and starting toward Billy.

Mo'Steel turned her around firmly. "Take a walk. You need to cool off."

Jobs didn't call a meeting. He had no interest in being in charge. And no less than an hour after Mother had disappeared into the drab gray sky, the others had gathered around where he was sitting with his back against a crumbling brick wall.

The wall made Jobs feel a little better. At least nothing could sneak up behind him. Jobs wasn't worried about the other Remnants, he was worried about — he wasn't sure *what* he was worried about. But he thought he'd heard —

I didn't hear anything, Jobs thought.

Billy was five feet away. He hadn't moved since Mo'Steel and the others dragged 2Face away from him.

Jobs had seen Olga taking Billy's pulse. She then sat down next to Mo'Steel and gave Jobs a sad shrug. "Billy won't be able to help us anytime soon."

"What's the matter with him?" Roger Dodger asked. The kid had someone's pink T-shirt wrapped around his head as a bandage. Blood was seeping through near his right temple. His eyes were droopy and dull, and he was leaned up against Violet for support.

"He's unconscious," Olga said.

"Thanks for the update." 2Face was standing, arms crossed, on the fringes of the group. "What we need to know is when — or *if* — he's going to wake up."

"I can't tell the future," Olga said mildly. "None of us can."

"Well *that's* pretty obvious," Anamull said with a meaningful glance at 2Face.

"This isn't *all* my fault," 2Face shot back. "Billy came down here because *he* wanted to. Jobs was the one —"

"Oh, please!" Mo'Steel exclaimed. "I was there. I saw you arguing with him. You knew exactly what you were doing."

"That's not how I remember it," 2Face said coldly. "And Billy is in no shape to back up your version of events."

"None of us is in any shape to do anything," Violet said. "Without the ship, we're — we're —"

"Dead," D-Caf said flatly.

"Hey — just calm down," Jobs said to the group. "Like Olga said, we can't see the future. I think we need to move beyond how we got here and talk about what we do next."

Silence.

Jobs felt his heart slow to a painful *thump, thump.* This group of people had been through tragedy and death and mind-boggling weirdness, and they'd rarely shown signs of giving up. Maybe they were brave or tenacious or just plain stupid.

And yet, now, they looked beaten. Jobs met Mo'-Steel's gaze and willed him to say something. Anything.

"Uh, we could start walking and look for some more water," Mo'Steel said hesitantly. "I mean, it's obvious we don't have enough."

Jobs felt like groaning. What they didn't need now was a panic over their pathetically small water supply.

"How much water *do* we have?" Roger Dodger asked, running his tongue over dry lips.

"Five and a half liters," Jobs said as evenly as possible.

A pause as that sunk in.

"Does anybody know how much you need each day to survive?" 2Face asked quietly.

"Maybe an ounce or two —" Olga started.

"Even in all this dust?" Violet asked.

"We should probably ration it," 2Face said. "Keep an eye on it."

"And who's going to do that?" Anamull demanded. "You?"

"I didn't say that!" 2Face yelled.

"We — might — find — more!" Jobs roared. That got everyone's attention. He continued in a quieter voice, "We could look in the Dark Zone —"

"I don't think we should just wander off," Violet said firmly. "What if Mother comes back and we're off on some wild-goose chase?"

"A wild goose? Yeah right," Anamull said harshly. "Did you forget that everything on this planet is dead?"

"What are we going to eat?" Edward asked. Jobs could hear the fear in his voice.

"Meanies," Anamull said.

Edward looked sick.

"I still think there may be food under the ash," Jobs said forcefully. "Maybe — maybe nothing living, nothing growing. But there may be something left from before the asteroid, the Rock, hit."

Jobs looked around at ten doubtful faces. He knew what he was suggesting was far-fetched. Maybe even ridiculous. But he needed *something*, some small hope for them to grasp. He couldn't let them lie down and wait for death.

"We've looked," D-Caf said harshly. "There's nothing in this ash."

They *had* looked. Jobs couldn't deny that. "Maybe — maybe we weren't looking in the right place," he suggested feebly.

"What could survive five hundred years?" Noyze asked gently.

"Freeze-dried food," Jobs said. "Like you'd take hiking. Beans. Maybe dried meal or flour. Canned goods. We could just dig. See what we find."

Violet was shaking her head. "The chances of finding anything are so small. And the energy we'd waste digging — it doesn't make sense."

"What do you want to do?" D-Caf asked Violet.

Jobs noticed D-Caf and Violet were sitting side by side, close enough to touch. Before, D-Caf would have been posturing with Anamull.

"Before" was before D-Caf had been hit by fléchette fire in a battle with the Meanies. Violet had brought him back to life by sharing a mutation she had kept hidden for who knew how long. She — this beautiful girl Jobs had once thought of as his girlfriend — could transform herself into thousands of carnivorous pea-green worms.

Jobs understood why Violet and D-Caf would have a bond; he was glad Violet had someone to talk to. But why wasn't Violet also hanging out with the others who shared the mutation, Roger Dodger and 2Face? Jobs shook off the thought. Jealousy seemed a little misplaced considering their situation. Still, he missed Violet. Missed what they used to have together.

"I think we should do as little as possible," Violet was saying. "Admit we're never going to survive on Earth, ration our water, sit still, and hope that Mother comes back."

"You really think Yago is going to save us?" Jobs asked doubtfully. Yago was a thieving egomaniacal snake. He'd probably already written them off as dead.

"Or Amelia?" Mo'Steel said with a bitter laugh. When Billy had control of Mother, the Troika — Amelia, Duncan, and Charlie — had repeatedly demanded they not return to Earth. The Remnants hadn't understood their demands and they certainly hadn't heeded them. Now Amelia and her buddies seemed to be getting even.

"Tate is up there, too," Violet reminded them.

Jobs said nothing for a moment, thinking about Tate who was kind and caring and imagining what Amelia and Yago might do to her. He suspected she was already dead.

"Billy might wake up," Noyze said quietly.

Anamull snorted. "You people are pathetic. If you want to sit around on your sorry butts spinning fantasies and waiting to die, fine. I'm planning to live. And I'm not turning my water over to *her*." Anamull pointed at 2Face. Then he raised his water bottle, uncapped it, and slowly drained the entire thing.

Jobs watched eagerly, enviously. He could imagine the cool sip of water wetting his tongue, his throat.

"That's your share of the water," 2Face said stonily. "You're not getting any more."

Anamull beamed an insolent smile at 2Face and then half ran, half danced over to Billy's still form. Mo'Steel reacted first — jumping up and running after him.

Jobs was moving to follow Mo'Steel when he heard the rustling again. A sound like dried palm leaves scuttling along in a gutter. What *was* that?

Mo'Steel and Anamull tussled over Billy's water bottle. Anamull came up with it. He stood up, holding the bottle over Mo'Steel's head and laughing as Mo'Steel jumped up and tried to grab it.

"Stop it!" Olga yelled. "That's enough!"

Anamull uncapped the bottle. He tilted up his face and opened his mouth.

"Anamull — don't!" D-Caf yelled.

"No!" Noyze yelled.

Violet and Edward were on their feet, rushing toward Anamull.

The water poured down, some of it going into Anamull's mouth, some of it splashing over his dusty face. Mo'Steel jumped up again and knocked the bottle out of Anamull's hand. It hit the ground and rolled, the rest of the water spilling and quickly vanishing into the ash.

Mo'Steel stormed off. Noyze went after him. Anamull wandered off in the direction of the dead Meanies. The others scattered.

The meeting was over.

Jobs scanned for Edward. He was okay, huddled down near D-Caf and Roger Dodger. Reassured, Jobs backed up and sat down again with his back against the brick wall.

No use denying it. He felt, he *knew* someone was watching them. Someone or some*thing*. Maybe whatever was watching was making that scuttling noise like dead leaves blowing in the wind. Maybe not. But Jobs was certain they weren't alone. Earth wasn't as empty, as dead as it looked. That's what he'd been hoping for. But somehow it wasn't a comforting thought.

(CHAPTER THREE)

HIS LIFE WAS VERY MUCH IN DANGER.

The clock chimed 12/60.

Echo barely registered it. She was drifting, day-dreaming as she always did while working. The clock finished chiming as she pulled her worn mat farther down the row, pulling her basket after her.

She knelt down in front of a row of stumpy plants. Her hands worked automatically, efficiently stripping the leaves and berries off and dropping them in her tightly woven basket. She left behind a row of fibrous stalks. These would be left to dry in the fields for another 30/24 and then harvested to make rope and material for clothes.

Echo hoped the elders would approve a new tunic for her out of this harvest.

Another 60/60 and she'd finish this row. Maybe sooner. The crop was poor. Anyone who'd studied food production could see the soil was overworked. Echo could feel the exhaustion in the soil's powdery texture, see it in the soil's washed-out color. The out-of-balance soil and paltry crop depressed Echo, depressed all the field-workers.

Woody had them working overtime calculating the effects of different fertilizing compounds, but so far nobody had discovered a solution. Woody even spoke of demanding a year's rest — a time when the entire colony would go into stasis, conserving energy and food until the soil was well rested.

Well, Echo thought, *soon we will learn if he has the nerve.* She doubted he did. Woody was a brilliant soil chemist but he didn't have what it took to stand up to Crutch. To be fair, none of the Alphas did. They were people of science. They couldn't be expected to argue with those — those primitives. Echo shivered. Soon they would be here, filling the colony with their vulgar laughter, strange animal smells, and stories —

"Echo!" came Westie's strident voice from the next row. "It's time for j'ou to sleep. Didn't j'ou say j'ou were going to keep a better eye on the time today? I'm a busy woman. J'ou can't expect me to mind j'our affairs."

"That's the only thing j'ou *can* expect," came Mattock's deep voice from the next row.

"What's that?" Westie called.

"I said — thanks for the reminder," Echo called, trying to keep the smile out of her voice. She put the berries she was holding into the basket and got to her feet.

"Leave your basket," Westie called. "I'll take it in."

Echo already had the load resting comfortably on her hip, but she reluctantly let it slide to the ground. She knew better than to argue with Westie, her master.

"Thank j'ou," Echo said evenly, hiding her irritation. She didn't want to sleep. It seemed that since she'd gone through the procedure to give DNA to help a new life be born in the lab, the others were always watching her every move. Wondering if she was okay. She didn't want Westie to have the satisfaction of adding Echo's basketful of leaves and berries to the pile in the storeroom.

She was tired of people ordering her around and insisting on doing her favors. Most of all, she was tired of elders telling her to rest but expecting her to fill her idle time with things that were supposed to help the colony — things like those maddening soil toxicity calculations.

Echo made up her mind as she strode down the row, collecting a wink from Mattock. She wouldn't go straight to her room. She'd go to the observation site near the storeroom. If anyone asked her what she was doing there, she would say she was preparing for the vote. That was not a lie.

Minutes later, Echo sighed with pleasure as she sat down in the faded, stained chair and fitted the goggles to her eyes. In the middle of the day, with everyone at work, the observation point was empty. For once, she wouldn't have to hurry, wouldn't have to observe the newcomers with Marina and India hanging over her shoulder and urging her to give them a turn. Maybe now she would be able to see the creatures Lyric wouldn't shut up about.

Echo quickly scanned the landscape. No creatures. That was the first thing she registered. She was beginning to think Lyric had imagined the two-headed things she'd been vividly describing for days.

Then Echo noticed something else that made her straighten her back in surprise — the ship was gone! And yet, the newcomers were still here. She could see her favorite one pacing not far from where the lens came aboveground.

He was clearly not a member of any of the tribes. He wore very fine clothes. Earlier, Echo had seen some of the newcomers with glittering silver containers of some sort of gas. On that day, they'd carried carefully worked tubes and masks so they could inhale the gas. But now this newcomer had laid his container and mask aside. Why?

And why did he look so nervous? Echo smiled to herself. Perhaps that was simply explained as a sign of intelligence. His life was very much in danger. He *should* be nervous.

Did he still have the bottle? Yes, Echo saw with great interest, he did. Mattock claimed to have seen the newcomers drinking out of these bottles. He thought the bottles were full of water. That was surely a fairy tale. Nobody could have that much water for their personal use. It was enough to plant a crop.

That evening the colony would meet to decide what should be done about these strange humans. Would they accept them into the colony or leave them to die on the surface? Westie had warned Echo that Woody would ask her opinion in the meeting. A mark of her newly elevated status.

After Frank had died unexpectedly last year when a beam in his laboratory collapsed, Echo had been chosen to give a new member her DNA.

Westie made no secret of the fact she had voted against the new birth. "Bringing a child into the world to starve is not proper," Westie had said coldly. Her words worried Echo — was the crop really *that* bad? — but Lyric said the old woman was just jealous. What if Westie was jealous enough to claim the baby had a genetic defect — even if it was perfect? Then the baby would be given away to the Marauders and Echo would see her only twice a year.

Stop it, Echo told herself. The baby won't be here for 6/30s. The meeting was tonight. She needed to concentrate on that.

What should she say?

She wanted the newcomers let in. The luxury of having eleven new people to talk to was practically unimaginable. Echo longed to hear the newcomers' stories. Where had they come from? How had they built their ship? She imagined long evenings listening to their storytelling.

But she couldn't stand in the public meeting and argue to admit the newcomers for their entertainment value. No, Westie had lectured her on this point often enough. Only scientific reasons were acceptable in meeting.

So she needed another reason. She'd promised Lyric she would be persuasive. So . . .

So.

So.

Echo watched the light-haired newcomer pace and her mind drifted. She began to wonder about the new life that was growing in the lab. She wondered whether it would be a boy or a girl. She hoped it would be a girl. A girl who looked at least a little bit like her.

She tugged her mind reluctantly away from these irrelevant thoughts. Better to think of the meeting, of what she would say.

Suddenly, Echo felt a smile spread slowly across her face. She knew what she would say at the meeting.

(CHAPTER FOUR)

"ALL WE NEED IS A PENCIL
AND A PIECE OF PAPER."

Violet sat on a crumbling step and scanned the horizon. Gray below, gray above. She wanted to find beauty in the ruined Earth, in the stark ash-filled landscape, but — well, it was difficult. Even the light was unchanging and dull and made her feel as if she were living life under cheap fluorescent fixtures.

Her eyes moved over the ashy ground until her gaze fell on Jobs. She'd been avoiding even looking at him, but now she gave in and stared. He was sitting with his back against a brick wall, a fléchette gun in his lap, lost in thought.

Violet wanted to talk to him.

But she couldn't.

Somehow she knew she had to keep herself apart. As far as Violet knew, Jobs was one of the few who hadn't been . . . *tainted* by a mutation. Jobs.

Mo'Steel. Olga. Noyze. They were the only ones who were unchanged.

Violet didn't feel worthy of Jobs's friendship anymore. Not since she'd told everyone about the worms.

D-Caf tapped her shoulder. "What's Anamull doing with those Meanies?" he asked, jutting his chin toward the horizon where Anamull's tiny form was just visible.

"No idea," Violet said wearily.

D-Caf snickered nastily. "Hey, Anamull finally found some friends who can appreciate him. They're *dead* friends. But I think they're still smarter than he is . . ."

Violet closed her eyes. D-Caf's feeble attempts at humor gave her an actual headache. He never stopped making stupid jokes. Violet longed for quiet, wanted to tell D-Caf to just go away. But she could sense the hysteria just below his goofy surface. He needed someone to help him understand what he'd become when she'd shared her worm-mutation with him.

And she was the only one who could do that.

Who else could figure out what might happen if he got out of hand? He might attack someone or he might go worm and never come back. . . .

No.

D-Caf was her responsibility now, her family, her albatross. Roger Dodger, too. Even 2Face. Violet had to ignore how she felt and embrace this new reality.

"Hey, Violet," D-Caf whispered, leaning too close. "I'm getting really thirsty."

"So drink some of your water."

"I'm saving it."

"Then try not to think about it."

Short pause. Too short. "Hey, Violet," D-Caf said thoughtfully. "Do you think we can survive without water? I mean, if we went worm? Could we live in the ash?"

Violet had been wondering the same thing. "I — I don't know," she admitted.

"If we could," D-Caf said slowly, "we might survive even if no one else does. In the end, it might just be you and me and Roger Dodger and 2Face."

"Let's not talk about that," Violet said softly. "Not yet."

"We — we could save the others," D-Caf said excitedly. "If they die of thirst . . . We could use the worms to bring them back."

"No," Violet said sharply.

"Why not?"

"We're not making any more — people like us," Violet said shortly, rubbing her temples.

"But —"

"D-Caf, please! And, *please*, just be quiet for a few minutes . . ."

"Okay, you don't have to bite my head off," D-Caf said, chuckling. "Get it? Bite — my — head — off! Guess you already did that, huh?"

Violet forced herself to smile and tried not to think about spending eternity with an idiot.

2Face looked at the others, scanning, hoping to find some angle she could work. What was her best chance at survival? Should she stay with the others or sneak off on her own? Which was a bigger danger — the harsh unknown environment or ten people who blamed her for getting them stuck here?

The wind picked up. Ash swirled around 2Face's body, clouding her vision. She heard something — something that gave her goose bumps. Moaning. A sound like the whole planet moaning. 2Face shuddered. She didn't want to be alone. Not here. She'd have to take her chances with the group.

And that meant she had to lay the blame for losing Mother on someone else. Who?

Jobs? He'd bought Yago's stupid trick. He'd believed the seedling Yago'd planted was real. If he hadn't, none of them would have been on the surface to be abandoned.

No, 2Face realized. She couldn't pin this on Jobs. The others looked to him as a leader. She couldn't take that security away from them. Too risky. They were close to hysteria. They needed Jobs to lean on.

Billy? He was unconscious.

Unable to defend himself.

2Face rocked slowly back and forth on her heels. She watched Billy. How could she have believed he was powerful enough to protect them? He should have watched Yago more carefully. He should have crushed Amelia while he had the chance.

Surely she could make the others see that.

"Jobs, come quick!" Mo'Steel called. "It's Billy!"

Jobs shook himself out of a half daze and scrambled to his feet. He felt for his water, his pistol. Both still there. Good. He ran the fifty feet to where Noyze, Olga, and Mo'Steel had gathered around Billy.

2Face was hanging back. Maybe she was afraid to approach the others after the way she had attacked Billy.

Or maybe she's waiting for the chance to stab us in

the back, Jobs thought grimly. He tried not to look at her as he joined the others.

Billy was sitting up with a strangely rigid posture. His eyes darted around wildly, flitted fantastically fast from Olga to Noyze to Mo'Steel — and then settled on Jobs. His expression was full of silent pleading.

Olga was down on her hands and knees near Billy's shoulder. "Have some water, Billy. It will make you feel better."

Billy's head jerked. His hand flashed through the air. His gaze never left Jobs's face.

Olga let the water bottle drop. She turned to give Jobs a questioning look.

Jobs knelt down next to Billy, remembering Billy had been unconscious ever since the ship had taken off. He was probably wondering where they were and what was happening.

"We're on Earth," Jobs told Billy in a quiet, soothing voice. "Mother is gone. We think Yago and Amelia took control of her somehow. Are — are you still connected to the computer? Can you bring the ship back?"

Billy's mouth began to move. Sound came out, but it didn't sound like speech. To Jobs, it sounded like the high-pitched squeaking of a rodent. Reading Billy's lips didn't work, either. They were moving way too fast.

"Slow it down, Billy," Jobs said.

Billy stopped talking. He paused, then tried to talk again. His words still came out garbled. His gaze never wavered from Jobs's face.

Noyze came and crouched down next to Jobs. She put a slim hand on Billy's shoulder. "I think he's out of time-sync somehow."

The expression in Billy's eyes seemed to confirm this.

Jobs nodded. "This happened before," he explained to Noyze. "When we first woke up on Mother. Billy was slowed down from the trip on the *Mayflower*."

"Well, now I think he's sped up from being connected to Mother," Olga said from over their shoulders. "Think about it. He must be used to processing a deluge of information."

"Makes sense," Jobs admitted.

"How did you — help him before?" Noyze asked.

"We didn't," Jobs said. "He just seemed to come out of it all on his own."

"Well, it's different this time," Noyze said. "We understand what's wrong with him. We should be able to think of a way to help."

Jobs nodded, feeling numb with — not *fear*, with *hopelessness*. He didn't have to communicate directly with Billy to know his connection with Mother had been broken. Otherwise, he would still be receiving a huge amount of information from her and would be okay.

Scritch. Scritch. Scritch.

There was that sound again. Jobs wondered if he should mention the noise, ask if anyone else had heard it. He decided not to bring it up. Not now, anyway. Not until they figured out what they were doing.

Billy, Jobs berated himself. *Concentrate on Billy.*

"All we need is a pencil and a piece of paper." Violet had joined them.

Jobs noted bitterly that D-Caf was slinking along beside her. As usual.

"Billy can probably still write," Violet said rationally.

"A *pencil?*" Mo'Steel asked incredulously.

Jobs had a sudden, miserable reminder of how Violet had been when he'd first met her. A Jane dressed in white lace. Her hair pinned up. She'd rejected technology; refused to use a link; discussed the stylistic differences between Bonnard and Monet. She probably even wrote with a pencil.

They'd come a long way since then. Traveled many hard miles on a twisted, sad trail. Jobs wished they could somehow go back to those people they'd been — scrubbed, whole, uncompromising.

"Come on, Mo'Steel," Violet said. "It doesn't have to be an actual pencil. A stick would do. A piece of pipe. Billy can write in the ash."

Suddenly, everyone was scrambling around, poking in the ash, looking for something Billy could write with.

Jobs didn't help. He didn't want to turn away from Billy. They stared at each other. Stared. Stared. And then Roger Dodger came up and put a piece of rebar in Jobs's hand. Jobs gave it to Billy and he started to write.

"What does it say?" Jobs asked.

Noyze moved around, craning her neck so that she was in a position to read. "It says —"

"What?" Jobs asked.

Noyze licked her lips nervously. "It says: Keep 2Face away from me."

Jobs lifted his head and met 2Face's gaze. "Back off," he said to her without a second thought.

2Face's expression hardened. She didn't move.

"I said — back off!" Jobs yelled.

After a tense pause, 2Face turned angrily and walked away. Once she was gone, Jobs crouched down next to Billy and whispered, "What about Mother? Can you bring her back?"

Billy flung the rebar away. He tucked his head under his arm and stayed that way.

(CHAPTER FIVE)

"I DON'T FEAR HER."

"Echo, what is j'our opinion on this matter?" Woody asked casually from his seat on the dais.

Echo shot a nervous glance at Lyric and slowly rose to her feet. The meeting hall was packed with all forty members of the colony — from Rainier, the doctor and the oldest elder (he was sixty-seven) to little India who was sitting on her mother's lap (she was three).

All of their faces turned up toward Echo and she felt her throat squeeze closed. This was her first time speaking in a public meeting and she felt very adult. Very adult and very nervous. To calm herself, she focused on the painting of her mother. It was part of a wall depicting every member of the colony right back to the first Generation. Echo's mother seemed to smile at her encouragingly.

"It is my opinion that we should welcome the newcomers to the colony," Echo said formally.

"May I ask how j'ou came to this conclusion?" Woody asked.

"Yes," Echo said. "I believe the newcomers could serve as an important DNA reservoir for the colony."

Woody studied her for a moment and then said, "Thank j'ou, Echo. We appreciate j'our contribution."

Echo sat, relieved to be out of the spotlight.

Lyric leaned close. "Nicely done."

But, up front, Westie was already waving her hand dismissively. "Unnecessary! We don't need the newcomers' DNA! We have enough for a dozen generations."

"A dozen generations will pass in time," Rainier said.

"If we're lucky!" Westie said hotly. "If we're lucky! We can't afford to think three hundred years ahead. This colony needs to worry about improving the next harvest. Unless we do that, we will starve. Even *considering* bringing eleven more mouths into the colony is foolishness."

"Blah, blah, blah," Lyric whispered in Echo's ear. "Borlaug says Westie can think of nothing but her own hunger."

"She's my master," Echo said in a warning tone.

"Yes, but she isn't Borlaug's master," Lyric said irritably.

"No, but still . . ." Echo said.

"Still *nothing*," Lyric snapped. "J'ou don't have to fear her."

"I don't fear her," Echo whispered angrily. "But I know she'll make my life miserable if she thinks I insulted her."

"Would j'ou two shut up?" Mattock asked, leaning over from Echo's other side. "I'm trying to listen."

"Yeah, shut up," Lyric said, sitting back and crossing her arms over her chest. "Borlaug is speaking. I want to hear this." Borlaug was the colony's head technician and Lyric's master. Lyric worshiped him and Echo guessed he *was* brilliant — if j'ou could ignore his bulbous head and beakish nose.

"They built that ship, so I say we let them in," Borlaug was saying. "They could help us with the Beasts — open up some of the other environments — then there'd be more food."

"Where would the water for more crops come from?" Westie challenged him.

"Maybe they could get the artificial rain system running," Borlaug said.

"That system hasn't worked since my grandfather was young," Westie said. "The Beasts — j'ou're dreaming."

"Speculating," Borlaug said with a dignified nod.

"They're armed," an elder named Ali Kosh said suddenly. "That's what worries me. That and the fact we know nothing of their genetic makeup. They could be violent. They could destroy the habitat we have rather than helping us win space from the beasts."

"They're bloated," Westie said. "Too much water. Too much food. I doubt they could ever adjust to our life of restraint."

Lyric leaned toward Echo. "Who is she to talk? I doubt she could adjust to a life of —"

"Shh," Echo told her.

"Nile," Woody said. "We've heard nothing from j'ou."

Nile was Lyric's mother. Many colony members went to her for advice. She was known for her quiet wisdom.

"I fear for our alliance with the Marauders," Nile said softly. "We have no way of knowing how they will react to these newcomers in our midst."

"That's it," Lyric whispered to Mattock and

Echo, sounding proud of her mother's great influence. "The newcomers will die on the surface."

And so it was. The elders discussed the issue for another 10/60 and then voted unanimously to leave the newcomers on the surface to die.

As they got up to leave the meeting, Echo's mind drifted to the light-haired newcomer who was always pacing. She was sad they would never meet.

"It's still early," Mattock said as they strolled away from the meeting. "Want to go to the observation point?"

"Sure," Lyric agreed.

Echo placed a hand on her forehead. "I — I think I'll go to bed."

"Do j'ou feel okay?" Lyric asked immediately.

"Just tired."

"Want me to come back with j'ou?"

"Why? So j'ou can watch me sleep?"

Echo turned toward the dormitory, not feeling at all tired. She opened the door to the empty dormitory and climbed into bed. *Maybe they'll be lucky,* she thought as she laid her head on the pillow. *Maybe the columns of burning gas will catch them while they're sleeping.*

(CHAPTER SIX)

"COULD BE GHOSTS, COULD BE *FOOD*."

There was no dusk, no nightfall. Weak sunlight continued to push through the haze of ash and provide a uniform gray light. Jobs wished for morning, a time to say "let's start over."

Not happening.

It was so easy to drift. To sit with his back against the wall, thinking sad thoughts and waiting for the end. Some part of Jobs wanted to let go, give up the fight.

But Edward.

Edward was just six. He didn't deserve this. A weird sense of duty gave Jobs the energy to pull himself to his feet and call everyone together near where Billy and Noyze were huddled down. Billy was unchanged; his movements were still jerky. He was still refusing to write.

They came reluctantly, bandaged, limping, faces

drawn with fear and doubt. 2Face held back, standing a few feet away from the others. Anamull didn't come at all. He was hunkered down a hundred yards away, next to the dead Meanies.

"Mo'Steel has an idea," Jobs told the assembled group. "We're going to try to modify the dead Meanies' suits and take them out to search for water. I've got to be honest with you: It's a long shot."

"It's worth a try," Mo'Steel said stoutly.

"What about Anamull?" Noyze asked, her dark eyes traveling to where the oversized teen stood guard over the Meanies. Anamull was glaring back at them like a rabid dog. "You think he's just going to let you have the suits?"

Jobs shrugged, even though he felt quite nervous about facing Anamull. "We're going to talk to him. Find out what he has to say."

"I'm going to continue to look for food in the rubble," Olga spoke up. "It's probably pointless but if anyone wants to help me —"

"I will," 2Face said.

Olga hesitated for a moment, and then nodded. "Thanks."

Jobs gave Violet an uneasy smile. "Violet, I thought you might want to stay here in case Mother returns."

"Yes, I would," Violet said.

"I'll stay with her," D-Caf said automatically.

"Fine," Jobs snapped, unable to hide his irritation with D-Caf and Violet's new friendship.

"I'd like to stay here, too," Noyze said. "In case something changes with Billy."

"Of course." Jobs looked at Billy's hunched form with great sympathy. Billy had saved their lives many times. Jobs hoped he wasn't blaming himself for his failure now. Maybe he just missed Mother, missed that weird connection. . . .

The group started to break up. Jobs beckoned Roger Dodger and Edward over to him. "I have a special job for you guys," he said quietly. "It may be very dangerous or it may be totally pointless. . . ."

"What is it?" Edward asked eagerly.

"Well . . ." Jobs hesitated and then plunged ahead. "I keep hearing — *something*." The two younger boys were listening to him earnestly and Jobs suddenly felt like a total fool. "It's probably nothing — could be the wind chasing something around but —"

"Tell us," Roger Dodger said impatiently.

"Okay, this sounds stupid, but I keep thinking I see — or *sense* — some sort of rats or mice scurrying around just out of view. I haven't actually seen them. But something is moving out there."

"Could be ghosts," Edward said matter-of-factly.

Jobs didn't answer. In this planet-sized graveyard with the wind howling, he couldn't really blame Edward for believing in ghosts. Some part of him felt he should object, that he should reassure his little brother, but he just couldn't do it.

"Could be ghosts, could be *food*," Roger Dodger said with a wriggle of his eyebrows. "We'll find a secluded spot, and wait for whatever it is. Come on, Edward. This is a perfect job for the Chameleon."

The two boys started off, talking excitedly about their assignment. Jobs sighed and went to find Mo'Steel.

Anamull watched Jobs and Mo'Steel moving toward him across the ash plain, bouncing slightly with each step. Earlier, when they were just here exploring, before that jerk Yago deserted them, Jobs'd said Earth's gravity was lower now. Something to do with the Rock.

Whatever.

But he'd done it, and now there were only two things of value in this place: food and water.

And, gross as it was, the dead Meanies were food. Before long, they'd all be down on their hands and knees begging him for it. Anamull couldn't wait. Couldn't wait to see them beg.

Especially 2Face.

Jobs and Mo'Steel had reached him now.

"Hi, Anamull."

Jobs sounded nervous and Anamull couldn't help but grin. This was it. The begging was about to begin. For starters, he wanted to make Mo'Steel and Jobs build him a fire. Anamull ran his fingers over the boomerang hanging from his belt as a sort of subtle threat, and then asked, "What?"

"We've come to get the Meanies' suits," Mo'-Steel answered coolly. "We're going to take them out to look for water."

Anamull's grin faded. This wasn't what he was expecting. For one thing, Mo'Steel hadn't mentioned eating the Meanies. For another, they hadn't asked his permission.

Jobs knelt and began feeling along one of the Meanie's metallic suits for the seam that would open it. He found it and split the suit open, revealing the Meanie's rubbery brown flesh. Mo'Steel bent to help Jobs. They pulled the suit free and dumped the soft, wrinkled Meanie into the ash.

Anamull frowned, surprised the Meanie was so puny. Suddenly, his prize didn't seem so impressive. He liked the Meanies better with their suits *on*. But Jobs and Mo'Steel had already turned to the second one and were pulling his suit free, too.

"Don't forget who got the suits for you," Anamull said angrily.

Jobs raised his head and frowned sternly at Anamull. "We haven't forgotten."

"Maybe you should pay some respect," Anamull said threateningly. "Ask my permission before you take the suits."

Mo'Steel and Jobs exchanged doubtful looks and didn't reply. They stood up, each holding one suit. Anamull considered his options.

He didn't want to go off looking for water. He wanted to hang out and wait for 2Face to crawl over and beg his forgiveness. Might as well let these boy scouts do the heavy lifting. He relaxed and gave Jobs and Mo'Steel a slow smile. "Good luck," he said slowly. "And don't forget — it's better to give than to receive."

"That went well," Mo'Steel said with amusement.

"Yeah," Jobs said dryly.

The two of them were dragging the Meanies'

suits across the ash plain toward the brick ruins where they planned to work. Jobs was thinking about the tools they had available — spades, shovels, a couple of boomerangs. Tools for digging, weapons. No screwdrivers, pliers, hammers, scissors. Nothing really — except for their own hands. *Good thing for the opposable thumb,* Jobs thought wryly. *It's the only thing we've got.*

"Let's rest a minute," Jobs said. In spite of their sleek appearance, the suits were surprisingly heavy and Jobs felt frail and frightened of hurting or stressing his body in this hostile environment.

Mo'Steel stopped walking but bounced impatiently on his toes. Neither one of them spoke for a moment. Then Mo'Steel shifted restlessly and said, "Come on. I can't wait to fly this thing."

"*If* we can," Jobs said cautiously. "These suits are built for Meanies. Our bodies are the wrong size, the wrong shape. The controls are meant to be operated with *tentacles.* And we really don't have those."

"You'll figure it out," Mo'Steel said with conviction. "Now come on. We're wasting time."

"Thanks for reminding me." The weight of responsibility was heavy on Jobs. He'd figure it out — or they'd all die of thirst. But hey, no pressure. Jobs pushed away the self-pity. No time for that now. There was only time to think.

Nobody came.

Anamull waited, rump in the ash. He tried to ignore the dry tickle in the back of his throat that was making him cough sporadically.

He waited.

Off in the distance, he could see Olga and 2Face poking around in the ash with their shovels. Noyze and Violet were sitting near Billy, talking. He could see their mouths move and, for a while, Anamull amused himself trying to figure out what they were saying. He was certain he'd seen Violet say his name more than once and he *thought* he'd seen her mouth say something like "cute."

Mo'Steel, Jobs, and the others were hidden from view.

He waited. Bored. Thirsty.

How long would this take? How long before the others got hungry enough to start thinking about Meanie meat? How long before 2Face started dreaming of a nice Meanie burger or some Meanie shish kebab?

One thing was sure: It was taking too long.

And another thing: Anamull hated to wait.

Always had. Back on Earth — wait, he was back on Earth. So: Back before the Rock, his teachers said he had ADD. Attention Deficit Disorder. Maybe they were right, because he had a definite deficit of attention right now. Staring at the wrinkly Meanies had lost its thrill way back. Actually, the things were starting to give him the creeps.

I need a little old-fashioned advertising, Anamull thought craftily. *A Meanie BBQ to get their mouths watering.*

A splinter of bamboo stuck out of the ash near his right knee. He reached forward to pull it free. The stick was bigger than he expected — about a foot long — and it looked like it would burn.

Anamull used the stick to stir the ash surrounding him. Could he find enough stuff to build a fire? Doubtful. The way this place looked, just about everything that could burn had burned long ago. But Anamull kept stirring. Nothing else to do.

He pulled up and tossed a glob of molten glass. Useless. He came up with handfuls of metal shards. Old screws? Whatever. He pushed the bamboo deeper. But there was nothing but ash.

CHAPTER SEVEN

"I'M INVINCIBLE."

Billy sat hunched down, his face turned toward a ruined wall. He blinked his eyes rapidly as the ash gray of the concrete warmed to royal purple and the constant twilight of the shadow zone gave way to flat fluorescent light.

He knew this place: Classroom 2 at Austin Second Central Congregational.

Billy knew he was dreaming. His first dream in a long time. While he was connected to Mother, he'd had no time for dreams. No synapses to spare.

He turned in a slow circle, taking in the details. High, waxed, gray linoleum floor marred by the occasional black sneaker streaks. Chalk smell mingling with the smell of scorched corn from the catering kitchen down the hall. Metal teacher's desk painted taupe. White plastic Swingline stapler. Jade plant in a green plastic pot. Valentines drawn with crayon on pink construction paper and taped to the dusty windows.

"Hello, Ruslan."

Ruslan. The name Billy's mother had given him. The name he'd had as a Chechnyan orphan — before he became an American, Big Bill's son.

Billy's dream-self spun. The voice came from Heather McMannis, fourteen years old and the prettiest girl in Billy's Sunday school class. She sat in the last row of student desks beneath a map of the Middle East, wearing a fuzzy pink sweater, faded jeans, cowboy boots.

Billy walked toward her, but before he could speak he let out the softest breath — and with that breath, Heather and the entire room blew apart into swirling dust, leaving Billy all alone.

Anamull labored for hours, slowly building a depressingly small pile of wooden and plastic scraps — charred branches, half-melted computer disks, telephone wire. Occasionally, he noticed Noyze or Olga glance his way. But nobody came over.

The Meanies kept him company. Watched him with their huge unblinking eyes. Didn't Meanies have eyelids? Anamull wondered. Apparently not. Too bad, because those eyes were raising the hair on the back of his neck. Twice he thought he saw them move. "Ignore it," Anamull told himself.

Anamull didn't have any matches. He didn't have a magnifying glass or a pair of glasses. The sun was weak. He didn't even have any decent kindling.

He thought for a moment. Then he took the bottom of his shirt and yanked hard. He placed the cloth gently on the ground and selected two bamboo slivers from his pile.

The wood was exquisitely dry. Anamull knelt down in the ash next to his nest and began to rub the wood slivers together, waiting for a spark.

"Can't we move this along?" Mo'Steel asked.

"No," Jobs said. "We have to do this right. Do it without getting hurt or breaking one of the suits. We can't go flying these things without knowing where the brakes are."

"Ooookay," Mo'Steel sighed.

Jobs sat back on his heels — he was squatting down in front of the Meanies' suits — and laughed in amazement. "Ooookay? We're looking at the real possibility of dying any second and you say 'ooookay'?"

Jobs was caught between aggravation with Mo'-Steel and relief that it seemed like *nothing* would ever change his best friend's personality. Mo'Steel was always impatient for an adventure, especially if the odds suggested he wouldn't survive it.

Mo'Steel shrugged. "This is taking forever."

"Well, we're almost ready," Jobs said. He was apprehensive about operating the Meanie suit, but he knew Mo'Steel would appreciate the action.

"Good," Mo'Steel said. "That'll be more exciting than making little squiggles in the sand."

"Sorry to *bore* you," Jobs said testily, "but do you remember what happened the last time I tried to work one of these things?"

"Vividly," Mo'Steel said with an amused smile.

Jobs had hit the button that fired the rockets when he'd hoped to launch a mini-missile, and the suit had shot off wildly like a punctured balloon.

That wasn't happening again. Especially not with Jobs actually inside the suit.

Jobs had carefully diagrammed the visible buttons in the Meanie suit — drawing in the ash with a piece of metal. All the buttons he could find, twenty of them, were in the long, thin tubes that covered the Meanies' tentacles. Sixteen in the right tentacle; four in the left.

Jobs leaned over his diagram and circled one of the buttons on the left side. "Start with this one," he said. "And remember — it could be the mini-missile."

"Okeydokey."

"Heads up!" Jobs yelled needlessly. Noyze, Violet, and the others had already taken refuge behind a massive chunk of concrete and rebar.

Mo'Steel crawled closer to the suit with an excited smile on his face. "Same old Mo'Steel," Jobs told himself, and almost believed it.

A spark.

Tiny. Glowing red in the eternal half-light.

Still rubbing his slivers of bamboo together, Anamull dropped the spark onto the cloth.

It died.

His arms — rock hard from a regimen of endless reps of bench presses in his parents' moldy basement — were numb with fatigue.

But he wouldn't let himself stop. He kept rubbing, rubbing, rubbing. Minutes passed, and then —

Another spark.

Anamull dropped it into the pile. The fabric caught fire, quickly shriveled up, and went out with a puff of foul-smelling smoke. Cursing, Anamull dropped the bamboo. He savagely kicked his pile of fuel, scattering it. Forget this! He rubbed his aching arms.

Forget it. He'd let 2Face make the fire when she came crawling.

He sat down in the ash and stared at the Meanies staring back at him.

Anamull got up. Forget waiting for 2Face. Time to try again.

Kindling. What could he use for kindling?

Birch bark would be nice. Or paper.

Paper . . .

Anamull patted his back pocket and felt the familiar lump there. He drew out his wallet and opened it. Nestled inside were three tens and two twenties.

P-money. The kind nobody used in 2011. But it *was* money, and everybody always took it in the end. He liked how annoyed the clerk got when he bought something with it.

Anamull shredded the bills into long strips, crumpled them together, and picked up the bamboo again.

"Which way are you heading?" Olga asked tensely.

"Into the Dark Zone," Mo'Steel said, squeezing his mother's hand and giving her a grateful smile. Grateful — because he was relieved she hadn't tried to talk him out of going. He had to go; they needed the water. But even if they hadn't needed it — he *wanted* to go. Riding an alien, rocket-powered space suit into subzero temperatures on an impossible mission to save his girlfriend and mother — it just didn't get better than that.

"Jobs says the Dark Zone is our only chance," Mo'Steel explained. "Go the other direction, we fry. 'Course, this way we have a good chance of going Popsicle."

Noyze squeezed his hand sharply, and he added, "Sorry, Mom. I didn't mean —"

Olga waved off the apology as if to say she was well aware of the danger he'd be in. "How long do you think you'll be?" she asked.

"I really don't know. Hopefully not too long."

"How do you know how long the rockets will last?" Olga asked. "Finding water won't be much good if you can't get back with it."

Mo'Steel was nodding his head to show his mother they'd thought of that. "Billy," he explained. "He knew — from being connected with Mother — he knew the Meanies' rockets last about twenty hours. We're assuming they were fully charged when the Meanies put them on."

"Why are you assuming that?" Olga asked abruptly.

"Just seems logical," Mo'Steel said. "Really, Mom, don't worry. Jobs has everything figured out."

Olga ignored his reassurances. "How will you keep track of time?" she asked doggedly.

"Jobs has a system," Mo'Steel said. "Don't ask me for details."

"But how will you find —" Olga's voice cracked, her eyes filled with tears, and she let the rest of the sentence trail off. Mo'Steel could see now how tense his mother was. She was waving her hands in front of her face as if to chase away the entire conversation.

"How will I find *what?*" Mo'Steel asked gently.

"Forget it, forget it," Olga said. "I trust you and Jobs. Just — just come back, okay?"

"Okay," Mo'Steel said easily. "Don't worry, Mom. Everything's cool."

Olga laughed shakily. "Cool? That's exactly what I'm afraid of!"

Mo'Steel shook his head at his mother's corny joke and let her wrap him in a tight embrace. "I'll be fine, Mom. I'll be fine," he said, as he hugged her back.

Two minutes later, Mo'Steel was walking with Noyze back toward where Jobs was waiting with the suits on the top of the stairway to nowhere.

Olga had gone ahead. Mo'Steel could see her talking to Jobs.

"That was weird," Mo'Steel said, trying to lighten the mood. "My mom isn't usually like that. She thinks scientists are supposed to be unemotional."

"She thinks she's saying good-bye to you," Noyze said. "Good-bye forever."

"Is that what you think?" Mo'Steel asked.

Noyze shook her head sadly. "So many things can go wrong."

"They won't," Mo'Steel said forcefully.

"How do you know?" Noyze was watching her feet, refusing to meet his gaze.

"I'm invincible," Mo'Steel said.

"That's ridiculous," Noyze said.

"I know," Mo'Steel told her. "But try to believe it. It might help."

Mo'Steel pulled Noyze into a gentle embrace. She felt so thin, so fragile. All bones — like a little bird. "Get some rest while I'm gone, okay? You looked exhausted."

"Nightmares," Noyze murmured into his shoulders. "Every time I doze off I have really creepy nightmares."

(CHAPTER EIGHT)

"LET'S RIDE."

"I look ridiculous," Jobs complained. "Worse, I *feel* ridiculous."

"Strap it up, Duck," Mo'Steel said. "You're styling."

Jobs looked down at himself doubtfully. His legs were shoved into the rear leg holes of one of the Meanies' suits. The front leg holes hung empty because his fingers were crammed into the part of the suit designed to hold the Meanies' tentacles. This was extremely uncomfortable, but it was the only way to work the controls.

His head was also covered by the suit — which made it difficult to talk. That was fine with Jobs. He'd already said good-bye to Edward. Now he wanted to go before Violet came over. Looking out of the oversized eyeholes, Jobs could see that she was standing with D-Caf. Everyone was there — everyone but Anamull — huddled at the top of a broken stair, waiting for Jobs and Mo'Steel to fly off on their desperate mission.

"Let me help," Noyze said, leaving Mo'Steel's side and approaching Jobs. She started fiddling with the seam that held Jobs's suit closed, sealing it up. "Maybe this will help keep you warm in the Dark Zone."

"Maybe it will keep this stupid thing from falling off," Jobs muttered nervously. He hadn't known the seam was open.

He noted with some surprise that he felt like throwing up. He was sweating. His hands were shaking. He tried to take deep breaths, tried to calm himself down. Deep breath in. Deep breath out.

"Let's ride," Mo'Steel said.

Jobs felt his stomach do a slow roll. "Ready." A pause. "You first."

Mo'Steel didn't hesitate. His suit suddenly shot into the air like an overgrown bottle rocket. Thirty feet — straight up. And it kept climbing.

"WOOLLY!" Mo'Steel's excited voice sounded very, very far away.

Jobs was just slow enough for Mo'Steel to get impatient.

Time to see what this baby can do, he thought giddily. He pressed the tiny button that sent him soaring straight up into the air, and kept pressing. The Meanie rockets responded with a gigantic burst of acceleration.

Mo'Steel shot up so fast his stomach dropped to his feet. He could almost feel the adrenaline rushing into his veins and he laughed out loud. He hadn't been this happy since — well, for a long time.

He held his finger steady. Quickly, surprisingly quickly, the faces looking up at him from the ground dissolved into blurry specks.

"Mo!" Jobs yelled angrily. "Mo, you idiot, come back!"

Mo'Steel left his finger where it was and Jobs's voice was almost instantly blotted out by distance.

He was high up now. Very high up. He thought he could almost see the edge of the Dark Zone. Could he go high enough to get out of the dust? Could he go right into space? Mo'Steel considered trying it just to see what would happen. He was sure the suit would be fine. One small problem: He didn't have any oxygen.

No oxygen in space would not be pretty. Mo'Steel knew how it would go: First he'd start to feel dizzy. Then he'd black out and his cold finger would slide off the button. Old man G would snag him —

Without warning, Mo'Steel flipped from *imagining* himself fall to *seeing* himself fall — it was the difference between watching a movie and being one of the characters.

In perfect, horrifying detail, he saw the ground rushing up, felt dusty air pricking at his eyes and making them water, heard wind roaring in his ears. He was picking up speed, picking up speed, picking up speed, kicking in panic as the distance vanished, arms windmilling, screaming, and —

Thud. Hitting the ground and knowing the pain for an excruciating second before everything went misty red and then black. . . .

Just as suddenly, the vision was gone. Mo'Steel was still climbing, his heart drumming, his throat half sealed with terror.

WHAT was that?

Shaking, his stomach cold with fright, he eased his finger off the button and began to descend. Slowly. Cautiously. His head pounding from an adrenaline headache.

Mo'Steel couldn't explain to himself what had just happened. It was like having a nightmare without bothering to fall asleep first. He wondered vaguely if he was losing his mind. He was grateful the Meanie suit hid his expression from Jobs.

"Enough playing around," Jobs said impatiently as Mo'Steel pulled up even with him. "We need to go. And I guess I don't need to tell you that you just wasted a bunch of fuel."

"Jobs —" Mo'Steel wondered if he should tell his friend what had just happened. Going into the Dark Zone was dangerous. Jobs was counting on him. He had a right to know if he was losing his mind.

"What?" Jobs asked irritably.

Mo'Steel heard the strain in his friend's voice. Maybe confessing wasn't the brightest idea. Another worry might push Jobs over the edge.

"Enough stalling," Mo'Steel said lightly. "Let's go." He promised himself he would hold it together long enough to get Jobs out of this mess. To get them all out, if possible.

The fire was burning.

It was small and foul-smelling and smoking, but it *was* burning. Anamull looked over at the Meanies, considering. . . .

Anamull drew out his Rider boomerang and approached the Meanies, averting his gaze from their eyes. He grabbed the end of one of the Meanie's legs — they didn't have feet; the end of the leg reminded Anamull of the top of a bowling pin — and plunged the boomerang in where the leg connected to the torso.

The blade slipped in much too easily and, before he could stop it, Anamull's hand followed it. His hand touched something wet and gooey and warm — hot! Pain! A searing, burning pain that made Anamull yank his hand back and curse violently.

He dropped the boomerang and staggered away from the Meanie.

"Awhhhh!" Anamull yelled, grasping his arm at the elbow and shaking it. His knees were weak and his stomach was tight — if it hadn't already been empty he would have thrown up. Vaguely, he realized his hand was covered in a glistening purple-black goo. He had to get it off. But how? He had no water, he'd already drunk it all, and there wasn't any more. His skin was blistering. An unpleasant chemical smell burned his nostrils.

Anamull took another step away from the Meanie. Some sort of reeking liquid was pouring from the cut he'd made. The Meanie was deflating like a balloon going flat, leaving only a thin layer of rubbery-looking skin behind. The liquid hissed as it sank into the ash.

The ash. The ash . . .

Anamull was letting out panicked, squeaky animal noises as he dropped to his knees and plunged his hand into the ash. The noises got even squeakier as he shook the goo-ash off in thick droplets, too scared to touch the stuff with his good hand. He dragged himself a few feet away, and plunged his arm into the ash again. His vision blurred and he fell onto his face. "Help," he muttered softly to himself before sinking into blessed unconsciousness.

2Face jerked awake and scrambled to her feet. She'd been dreaming of the worms. The worms inside her — baking in the hot sun, shriveling up from lack of water, turning to dust . . .

When had she fallen asleep? She hadn't meant to, but she was so woozy. . . .

Hunger. Hunger was making her weak. Making her have nightmares.

Something woke her. Her heart was pounding. She was short of breath. Her senses sucked in data.

Billy? Billy was okay. He and Noyze were huddled down fifty yards away. That was about as close as 2Face could get without Billy freaking out.

No smoke. No fire. No flaming pillars of gas — So what —

Screams.

Not frightened ones. Outraged ones.

Olga.

She was over near Roger Dodger and Edward. Over by that tall brick chimney that had somehow survived the devastation. 2Face could see her stomping around and examining the ground. She got to her feet, brushed herself off, and moved toward Olga. "What's wrong?" she called.

"My water is gone!" Olga yelled.

2Face automatically felt for her own bottle. It was still there, clipped to her belt. She let out her breath. If someone tried to steal her water, she'd — and what if Olga wanted —

"What do you mean — gone?" 2Face asked shakily.

"Gone — as in no longer here, vanished, poof," Olga said irritably.

"The bottle, too?" 2Face asked, fighting to make sense of the situation.

"Of course the bottle, too!" Olga shouted.

"Did you see anything?" Violet asked, as she joined them. D-Caf was shadowing her as usual. He didn't seem aware of the pained expression on Violet's face whenever she noticed him nearby.

"Sleeping," Roger Dodger said sleepily.

"Me, too," Edward admitted.

"Doesn't matter," 2Face said, tamping down the

cold fear that was trying to rise up from her stomach. "It had to be Anamull."

There was a pause as that sunk in. Nobody denied it. They all turned to look toward Anamull and the Meanies. He was still there — maybe a hundred yards away — far enough so that he couldn't hear what they were saying but close enough so they could see him. 2Face squinted into the distance. Anamull was lying down, probably sleeping.

"When was the last time anyone spoke to him?" Olga asked.

Nobody said anything as they thought it over.

"It must have been Jobs and Mo'Steel," Violet said thoughtfully. "When they got the Meanies' suits. I wonder what he's thinking —"

"About stealing water, obviously," 2Face said impatiently. "He did it before and he'll do it again unless we do something to stop him."

Olga and Violet both wore pinched, pained expressions that grated on 2Face's nerves. Why did they refuse to see what was staring them in the eye?

"I guess we need to post a guard," Violet said doubtfully.

Olga turned to look off into the distance. "I don't see any footprints in the ash," she said. "Maybe we shouldn't jump to —"

"We could just scare him," D-Caf said eagerly. "Scare him so he won't come near us."

"Not good enough," 2Face said coldly. They had to *deal* with Anamull, not play around.

Olga turned, her face angry. "What exactly are you suggesting we do?"

"Get rid of him," 2Face said, fighting to sound calm and rational. "Under the circumstances, I think stealing water means he's on his own."

"Why don't we just go talk to him?" Olga asked in measured tones. "Ask him if he took the water."

"We'd lose the element of surprise," 2Face said.

"Well," Olga said doubtfully, "this isn't exactly a military campaign."

"Besides, he could be dangerous," 2Face added quickly. "He has a boomerang and maybe a gun. I'm not willing to take chances."

"2Face," Olga said quietly. "I know you're scared, but I — I think we need to support one another now. I certainly don't feel any need to — to push anyone toward the end."

"I'm *not* scared," 2Face whispered furiously, backing away. Her foot hit something sticking out of the ground and she kicked it angrily away. "But if he touches my water, he'll regret it."

(CHAPTER NINE)

EATING, EATING, EATING.

"Let's just scare him," D-Caf said again after 2Face had stumbled away. 2Face was losing it — which was fairly amazing considering how tough she was — but he couldn't think about that now.

Scaring Anamull took his mind off his terrible thirst. He'd been trying to avoid drinking his water, taking just a tiny sip whenever he couldn't stand the scratchy feeling in his throat for another second. But maybe that wasn't a good plan. Not if Anamull was going to steal it before he could drink it —

"I can do it," D-Caf told Violet.

Violet and Olga were giving him doubtful looks. He couldn't tell how Edward was reacting; he could hardly see Edward. But Roger Dodger was smiling at him. Roger Dodger understood. They were buddies. They were I've-been-dead-and-now-I-have-the-wormy-mutation buddies.

"I know exactly what to do," D-Caf insisted. "I'll go worm and surface near Anamull. As a warning, like. So he'll know if he bugs us again, we'll — we'll let the worms protect us. What do you think, Violet? Is it a good idea?"

Violet took a moment to reply. "You've never let the worms out," she said. "You — might not like it."

"I want to," D-Caf said immediately.

Actually, it surprised him just how much he wanted to do it. In the beginning, right after Violet gave him the mutation, he'd had to concentrate to even feel the worms. He thought of them as sleeping, dormant.

D-Caf wasn't certain when that had changed. It must have happened slowly, without him really noticing. And now . . . He'd never admit it to the others, but the worms inside him wanted out. Desperately. The urge to let them out was even stronger than his thirst.

"Let's do it," Roger Dodger said.

"Yeah, why not?" Violet said, caving much more quickly than D-Caf expected.

Olga looked uncertain, but didn't argue. D-Caf was getting a weird vibe from her. Was it — fear? Was she actually afraid of the worms? Well, there was no need because he'd never hurt her. Never hurt anyone. He just wanted — needed — to let the worms out.

"I'm going to do it right now," D-Caf said excitedly.

Violet didn't say anything. Didn't smile. That worried D-Caf for a second, but it was already too late for worries, because somehow he'd released the worms and they were surging up with a painful force that made thinking about anything else impossible.

D-Caf began to whimper as the worms took over. They gained strength, gained strength — and then surged out.

The pain . . . unreal. Unlike anything D-Caf had ever known.

He was still there, still conscious, crying, wishing for it to stop, stop, stop, as the worms raced under his skin, rippling it. Until the pain disappeared because the human D-Caf no longer existed.

He was a million mouths attached to a million little bodies. Millions of bodies that were little more than short tubes.

Eating, eating, eating.

The thirst calming, the hunger growing more manageable.

Time passed, and somehow — he had no idea how — D-Caf gained control over the worms, forced them down, and became himself again . . .

He expected to see Anamull, staring down at him with masked horror, with his stupid, big-guy bravado. But instead, it was Violet and Olga and Roger Dodger. And the horror was unhidden, close to the surface. Something was very wrong.

"What happened?" D-Caf demanded. "Is it Jobs and Mo'Steel? Did they come back while I was — was gone?"

"Don't you know?" Olga asked.

Violet took a step away from him. "He doesn't, he couldn't — I don't think, I can't remember —"

"What?" D-Caf demanded, feeling the hysteria rise in his chest. Something was hideously wrong.

"He's gone," Roger Dodger said, wide-eyed. "Your worms got him. We ran to help — but it was too late."

D-Caf heard what Roger Dodger said, but he was distracted by something else. He'd just realized he wasn't thirsty anymore. He let out a low moan like an animal caught in a trap and began to run away. He was so ashamed. He couldn't stand to have them look at him that way.

* * *

"I'm going after him," Violet said, her voice filled with dread.

"Are you sure?" Olga asked anxiously. "It might be — too dangerous."

"Dangerous?" Violet repeated, furious. "Why? Because he might go worm again and get *me*?" She laughed harshly. "I made him what he is, Olga!"

Violet could have said more, but Roger Dodger was watching her. She could only guess what the kid was thinking.

She stopped talking and ran after D-Caf. She'd never liked the pudgy, nervous kid but now they were bound together. Family.

His footprints were clearly visible in the ash. Violet followed them until she found D-Caf huddled up behind a smashed-out neon sign. He was crying.

Violet steeled herself, approached him, and lay a hand on his shoulder. "Wasting water," she said.

"I — I have it to waste now," D-Caf muttered. "I have extra."

Violet sighed and knelt down next to him, trying to think of something comforting to say.

"It wasn't the way I imagined it," D-Caf said. "The — the worms just took over. You — you've got to tell me how to control them."

Violet thought about how to respond to D-Caf and decided on the truth. "I'm not sure I know how," she said calmly. "The few times I went worm, what I wanted to do was the same as what the worms wanted. I've never tried to resist them."

"Then I'm never letting them out again," D-Caf said fervently. "I think they might not let me come back."

Violet was relieved to hear this. If D-Caf pretended his mutation didn't exist, maybe she could do the same. "How did you get back this time?" she asked.

"I'm not sure, but I think the worms got scared." D-Caf seemed to be recovering from his fright. Some of the color had come back into his face.

"Scared? Scared of *what?*" Violet had never been aware of any emotion on the worms' part — and she doubted they were capable of it.

D-Caf didn't answer right away. "I think —" he said slowly, seeming to struggle with the memory, "I think they sensed something strange underground. A — a void."

"A void?" Violet asked. "You mean, a hole?"

"Yeah," D-Caf said, closing his eyes as if to concentrate better. "A big one. A place where there's no earth —"

Violet shrugged. "That could be anything. A parking garage or a cave."

"I guess," D-Caf admitted.

Violet sighed impatiently. This was one of the things that was so irritating about D-Caf. He made everything seem more important than it really was.

"Come on, let's go back," Violet said, holding out her hand.

D-Caf reached out his hand with a shaky, tentative smile. "Thanks, Violet. You're — a good friend."

Violet forced a smile, and was relieved when D-Caf didn't notice her lack of enthusiasm.

Edward was on patrol.

Roger Dodger had wanted to come with him, but Edward had slipped away and climbed the brick chimney alone, fitting his hands and feet into places where the mortar had fallen out. About fifteen feet up, he'd found a comfortable V to sit in and settled down.

Edward wasn't sure he wanted to be Roger Dodger's friend anymore. Roger Dodger could go worm, just like D-Caf.

Edward shifted his weight — the bricks weren't very comfortable to sit on — and scanned the horizon.

No rats.

No ghosts.

No sign of Jobs and Mo'Steel.

Edward wanted his brother. He knew he was probably safe on top of his chimney — nobody could see him unless they spotted his rifle — but he was lonely. And scared.

What if Jobs never came back? The thought was so frightening that it made Edward's stomach twist painfully. His mommy and daddy were gone — and that meant his brother could die, too.

Olga? Maybe Olga. She was nice, but Edward really wanted his brother back. He really —

Something moved. Over near the brick wall.

Reflexively, Edward looked up. At first, he thought he'd actually spotted the rats or whatever. Jobs would be so excited —

Something *was* moving, but it wasn't rats. It was — people. And not the ones he knew, either. Not anybody from the ship. People! Four, five, six — about a dozen of them!

Edward's heart began to hammer. He scrambled down the chimney and ran lightly in the direction the people were heading. He wanted to follow them. There weren't supposed to be any people here. If there were people that meant there must be food somewhere — and water.

Edward wanted some water. He was very, very thirsty. It wasn't just that his mouth was dry, he felt thirsty in his *bones*.

He tried not to make a sound because he didn't want the people to hear him sneaking up behind them and catch him. They could be dangerous or mean. He hugged the brick wall as he ran. He came to a corner, peeked around it — and there they were! Ten feet ahead of him.

Edward crept forward, keeping them in view, examining them from behind. They looked like — dust people. Their hair was matted with ash and their strange, crude clothes were dusty with it. They kept close together and moved through the ruins quickly and silently.

Edward's attention kept going to the shortest one — the one who was just a little taller than he was. He was wearing a patched-together leather coat. Was it a kid? Maybe they could be friends . . . Edward wanted to rush out and say hello, but he forced himself to stay hidden. He watched as the strange band of people pulled up an old sewer grate and disappeared underground.

They'd been gone twenty seconds before Edward dared to take a deep breath. People! It was unbelievable! Wait until he told Jobs. That is, *if* Jobs made it back. He *had* to make it back. . . . Especially now!

CHAPTER TEN

HOW HAD THEY LOST SO MANY PEOPLE?

Echo stood with Westie, Mattock, and Woody and surveyed their work. The entire harvest of berries and leaves had been brought out of the storeroom, carefully weighed out into equal halves and displayed in two plastic bins — one white, one red — on a table in the center of the exchange room.

"Which one do j'ou think they'll pick?" Woody asked.

"Red," Echo said.

"White," Mattock said at the same time. He spun to face Echo, his eyebrows raised in amusement. "Want to bet?"

"I'm willing," Echo said. Betting on the Marauders' bin selection was a traditional colony amusement. Almost part of the exchange ritual.

After more than five hundred years and over a thousand exchanges, the whole event was highly ritualistic. Tradition dictated the placement of the bins, the time of the Marauders' arrival, who stood next to who in the exchange circle, and dozens of other details.

Echo loved the traditions. Without question, the two exchanges were the most interesting days in the Alphas' 365/24. The most interesting *and* the most important.

Food for water; water for food. Without the exchange, the Alphas would die of thirst and the Marauders would die of hunger. The simple exchange had allowed their two groups to survive in an environment that supported little life.

"What's the wager?" Echo asked.

"7/24s of bathroom duty," Mattock said.

Cleaning bathrooms was not Echo's favorite chore, but she didn't want to disappoint Mattock. "14/24s," she said.

"Don't be foolish," Westie cut in irritably. "It doesn't matter which bin they pick. Each one contains exactly the same amount of food."

A pause. Then Mattock said brightly, "Good. That must mean we're finished here. Come on, Echo. Let's go get ready. We want to look our best for our guests."

"For the Marauders?" Westie said with a sniff. "How ridiculous."

"Go on," Woody said. "Go."

Echo and Mattock fled up the corridor. "I don't know *how* j'ou stand Westie," Mattock complained. "She's the most uptight, humorless, bitter —"

"Please," Echo said with a smile, "don't ruin my mood for tonight."

"Oh, I'll let the Marauders do that," Mattock said with false gravity. "That lovely smell they have should do it. And if that doesn't work, then there's the scars and scabs and extra body parts —"

"Extra body parts?" Echo repeated. "I've never seen any extra body parts."

"J'ou can't see much with all those clothes they wear," Mattock said, his eyes bright.

"I just hope something exciting has happened to *them* in the last 182/24s. We could use some entertainment around here."

"Oh, I don't know," Mattock said, pinching up his face and doing a fairly good imitation of Westie. "Entertainment has never done anything to increase the yield."

"Forget the yield," Echo said.

"Shocking language," Mattock said, maintaining his Westie voice. "Just shocking."

Echo was smiling as Mattock peeled off and disappeared into the men's dormitory. But her smile faded as she continued down the hallway.

The yield.

She'd devoted her entire life to the stupid *yield* — planting seeds, tending plants, watering, pruning, fiddling with soil composition, taking readings, making reports, watching, worrying, harvesting, weighing — and then starting all over again.

Maybe she couldn't hope for more. She was already 16/365s old. Probably too old to change. But what about her baby? Could the baby hope for nothing more than a life spent underground, in artificial light, worrying about the yield?

Somewhere between the men's dormitory and the women's, a wave of melancholy washed over Echo. She entered the cramped room with her shoulders slumped, all pleasure in the Marauders' imminent arrival forgotten.

"What happened to j'ou?" Lyric greeted her. She was sitting on her bunk, already dressed in her finest clothes. She'd woven bright pieces of cloth into her hair.

"Still tired," Echo said flatly.

"Are j'ou okay?" Lyric asked with what sounded like scientific curiosity.

Echo nodded. "A baby with my DNA is being developed in the lab to come into a life of drudgery. A life underground. Worrying about the yield."

"Well, cheer up," Lyric said lightly. "Maybe she'll be deformed and have to go live with the Marauders."

"Maybe that wouldn't be so bad," Echo said fiercely. "Marauder children play with toys, not soil toxicity samples. I don't want the baby to spend her life *composting*. I want her to do interesting things."

A flash of anger passed over Lyric's face, reminding Echo of the secret they shared, reminding her that Lyric couldn't afford to joke about deformities. " 'Interesting' things? Like what — battling Beasts?"

"I — no." Echo felt ridiculous discussing this with Lyric, of all people. And she didn't really want the baby taken by the Marauders. She'd only get to see her twice a year. "Forget it," she said dully.

Echo forced herself to put her strange feelings aside. She needed to be calm for the ceremony. From the time she was a baby, Echo had been taught that trembling hands or a nervous giggle during the exchange could endanger the entire colony. Above all, they must do nothing to raise the Marauders' suspicions that they were being cheated in any way.

A little before the clock chimed 12/24, Lyric and Echo left the dormitory together and joined the colony members gathered in the hallway outside the exchange room. As the clock began to chime, Woody pulled the door open and they filed in.

The Marauders entered the room through another door at the same moment. As the two groups came together to form a circle and join hands, Echo reminded herself to remain serene so the Marauders knew she had nothing to hide.

Woody stepped into the center of the circle for the beginning of the exchange. He was joined by one of the Marauders — a large bald man who was missing his two front teeth. His clothes were ill-fitting and matted with dust and filth.

"Thank j'ou for being our hosts," the Marauder said in a booming voice, leering strangely. He had wild, dangerous eyes and a huge dimpled nose sharp enough to be a weapon.

"Th — thank j'ou — for being our guests," Woody said, doing a very poor job of hiding his surprise.

Crutch — a wizened old man with a dense gray beard who had been the Marauders' leader ever since Echo was a little girl — was missing. That could only mean he was dead. The man who had joined Woody in the circle was called Hawk. Clearly, he was the Marauders' new leader.

Echo could see her own shock mirrored in the faces of the Alphas around the circle. Her heart bumped uncomfortably as her eyes traveled over the band, counting them.

Twenty.

Only twenty. At the last exchange, there'd been twenty-four. Four deaths in one 182/365. How had they lost so many people?

The Marauder women looked exhausted, Echo thought. Several of them had half-healed wounds or bruises visible on their faces and arms. She was relieved to see they still carried the traditional pouches of water. Whatever had befallen them couldn't be too bad if they had managed to make the collection.

Echo's shock slowly began to give way to a sort of cautious excitement. The Marauders would certainly have an interesting story to tell! She longed for the exchange to end so that she could hear it.

"We — we have grown this food with water j'ou provided and divided it equally into two bins," Woody said, struggling on with the ceremony despite his obvious confusion. "Please choose the bin that pleases j'ou and we will gladly take the other."

Hawk approached the table, and stuck his nose

disgustingly close to first the red bin and then the white. He took his time, seeming to consider. "We will accept the red bin," he said with that same disturbing smile.

"And we will gladly —" Woody started.

"*And* half of the white one," Hawk interrupted, his smile suddenly vanishing.

Woody stared at him stupidly. Halfway around the circle, Westie gasped loudly. Echo suddenly found it difficult to breathe. Lyric squeezed her hand painfully hard. The Marauders' expressions were hard; their hands were on their weapons.

"Our agreement is centuries old," Woody said with difficulty. His face had flushed an unhealthy purple.

"All of the red bin and half of the white one," Hawk said mulishly.

Echo could see a vein beating in Woody's forehead. "I need — can we have some time to discuss j'our — request?" he asked haltingly. "I must — consult with the other elders of our colony."

"J'our elders can consult," Hawk said derisively. "And since my band has no need for consulting but is content to follow my orders, we will hear a story while j'ou are away."

Hawk gestured impatiently to one of the younger Marauder men. "Tell," he ordered.

The man called Sanchez stepped into the circle. Woody stood there looking confused for another moment. Hawk hadn't even mentioned the water that was the Alphas' payment, Echo thought in dull amazement. Woody moved toward the door. Hesitantly, Westie, Rainier, Borlaug, and Ali Kosh followed him.

CHAPTER ELEVEN

"ANY OTHER QUESTIONS?"

"How much time?" Mo'Steel called, his voice muffled by the ill-fitting Meanie suit. He was ahead of Jobs, leading the way.

"An — hour and a half," Jobs called hoarsely. His throat was dry enough that shouting was difficult, painful. His tongue felt like a piece of meat — huge and swollen and alien. As soon as his hands were free, he planned to drink the last gulp of water in his bottle. "We have to — turn back in an hour — and a half or —"

"Right," Mo'Steel called, sounding distracted.

As they flew on and Jobs concentrated on making his numb fingers work, he heard Mo'Steel mumbling to himself. He thought he made out the words "five thousand four hundred." Was Mo'Steel calculating how many seconds they had before they had to turn around? Jobs felt a cold lump of fear swelling in his stomach and made a firm decision to ignore it. So Mo'Steel was acting a little strange. Under the circumstances, acting strange was normal.

They'd been searching for more than eight hours, heading straight toward the Dark Zone, the temperature dropping with each mile they traveled and all they'd seen was rubble.

The hugeness of the destruction made Jobs numb. He'd spent the long hours scanning the horizon for any man-made object that may have survived the Rock — or been built in the five hundred years since it hit.

He'd seen none. No intact buildings or water towers or electrical poles. Nothing but a flat plain of ash with the occasional ruined wall or stair still standing. There was no sign of lakes or rivers or oceans. Jobs had allowed himself to hope that as they got closer to the Dark Zone. . . . But no —

They were going to have to go back empty-handed. Go back and tell the others all they had discovered was frozen ash. They'd have to tell the others they were going to die of thirst. Go back and crush their last hope for survival.

Jobs wasn't sure he had the guts to stand in front of them and speak the truth. To face Olga's disappointment. Violet's. Edward's. Edward was only six.

Too young. They were *all* too young to perish. And 2Face. Somehow the idea of selfish, power-hungry 2Face dying after she'd fought so bitterly to survive made Jobs incredibly sad.

"Duck, look," Mo'Steel suddenly shouted. He gestured with the tentacles on his suit toward the horizon. "You see that?"

Jobs saw what he first took to be a solid wall about a mile or two distant. Then he noticed the swirling eddies — light gray, pewter gray, yellow-gray — churning, combining, separating and combining again.

The sight was somehow familiar, but it took his brain a minute to provide the proper memory: a storm. A storm the way it looks when you're coming toward it down the highway.

"Looks almost — like a tornado," Jobs called ahead, still fighting his oversized, dry tongue and the chilled muscles in his face.

"Ash tornado," Mo'Steel said.

"Maybe we should —"

"Whoa!" Mo'Steel yelled, and Jobs saw his head jerk in surprise. A flash of lightning had just brightened the swirling cloud. A boom of thunder reached them seconds later.

Jobs kept his eyes on the storm. For a second,

he'd thought he'd seen — through the swirling dust — no, it was impossible. But his heart was beating fast and he prayed for another lightning strike so he could see —

The flash came.

Jobs saw — something. Something that looked like — well, it looked like *San Francisco*. Not just a few buildings but *everything*: the skyscrapered down-town, the sweeping bay and the rust-red Golden Gate Bridge. All of the buildings were intact; the electric lights twinkled merrily.

Joy swelled in Jobs's chest. "Mo!" Jobs shouted jubilantly.

"Yeah?"

But in the few seconds it had taken for Mo'Steel to respond, Jobs had realized it couldn't be. He'd seen San Francisco wiped out by a chip, a pebble that had spun off the Rock and hit before the *Mayflower* had left Earth.

Jobs studied the distinctive roofline of the AOL tower and told himself it wasn't there. He'd seen the city's skyscrapers, including the AOL building, knocked over like toys. Seen the Golden Gate wrap around the U.S.S. *Reagan*. Seen the water of the bay transformed into a vast column of superheated steam.

What he was seeing now was some sort of cruel joke. A mirage, a hallucination. San Francisco was gone. There was no way he'd ever be able to forget that.

"What do you want to do?" Mo'Steel shouted.

"I — do you —" Jobs couldn't bring himself to ask Mo'Steel if he saw the city. With an incredible force of will, he bowed his head so that he couldn't see the glittering lights. "Let's turn back!" he shouted. "Storm looks bad."

If Mo'Steel can see San Francisco, he'll say something now, Jobs told himself. *Please let him say something —*

"You're the boss," Mo'Steel shouted. Without even glancing back toward the storm, Mo'Steel turned his suit around.

He doesn't see it, Jobs told himself with infinite sadness. He looked at the ghost city one more time, wrenched his eyes away and turned his suit toward camp and the burden of delivering the worst kind of news.

"Excellent!" Hawk boomed when Sanchez finished his story — a long, violent tale about the Beasts attacking Crutch and killing him.

Echo, Lyric, and Mattock had withdrawn to the

corner of the room. Even after her long 30/24s of waiting, Echo could only pretend to listen to the storytelling. Her mind was consumed with trying to figure out how they could stop the Marauders from stealing their food.

Hawk motioned to one of his band — a girl named Grost who walked with a slight limp. "Bring me my sack!"

Grost took a small pouch from around her neck and began to nervously unwind the closure as she moved stiffly toward Hawk. Hawk roughly grabbed the pouch out of her trembling hands and took a deep swig.

"What is it?"

"Stay on guard," Echo whispered tensely. "Be ready to fight."

Mattock goggled at her as if she'd grown a third eye. "Fight with what? They're armed. We're not."

"What about the other nineteen of them?" Mattock whispered, clearly shocked by the very idea of fighting.

"Do j'ou want to starve?" Echo demanded, unintentionally letting her voice rise. She saw one of the Marauders — an elder named Aga — glance their way and smile, apparently at their discomfort.

Suddenly, the Alpha elders opened the door and

were filing back into the room. Woody came first, and the smile he offered Hawk did little to hide his grim mood.

Hawk clapped his hands together and laughed. "What has the *committee* decided?" he asked derisively.

Woody straightened his spine and faced Hawk squarely, making Echo feel proud of him. "We would like to consult with the entire colony."

Hawk sucked his teeth and grinned. "No," he said slowly.

"No?" Woody asked, taken aback.

"No," Hawk repeated, his face losing its joviality. "J'ou don't need to discuss it with the entire colony because there's nothing to discuss. J'ou must accept my offer or die."

Woody's face had gone purple again, but he stood firmly in front of Hawk's wild gaze. "Kill us and j'ou will die, too," Woody said.

"No," Hawk said almost gently. "We will keep enough of j'ou alive to work for us. Just enough to plant the crop and harvest it."

Now Woody's strength seemed to leave him. His knees began to shake and he took a step away from Hawk. "J'ou are giving us the choice of dying by the sword or from starvation," he murmured.

Hawk smiled kindly. He stepped forward and grasped Woody's shoulder, steadying him. "No," he said again, "I'm not giving j'ou a choice at all."

Woody's knees buckled. At first, Echo thought he'd collapsed from a heart attack, but then she realized that there was something sticking into his chest.

"J'ou stabbed him!" Echo shouted, pointing a shaky finger at Hawk. She rushed toward Hawk, stunned, horrified, her fists beating in the air.

Hawk turned casually away as someone grabbed Echo's arms and pinned them behind her. She lashed out, kicking her legs wildly, screaming, fighting to get free. She twisted — expecting to see a Marauder restraining her — but it was Mattock and Borlaug holding her back.

Rainier — the colony's doctor — was kneeling at Woody's side and shaking his head in amazement. "He's gone. Gone already."

Hawk spun back, his bloodshot eyes glowing with pleasure. "Poisoned blade," he said sweetly. "Any other questions?"

"No," Westie said, her voice remarkably calm. "No questions. We'll give j'ou what j'ou ask."

CHAPTER TWELVE

"YOU LEFT ME."

The smells came to Mo'Steel first. Warm kitchen smells that blocked out the bad-breath-and-sweat stink of the Meanie suit. The hot, dry smell of an oven heating, the earthy smell of yeast rising and the medicated tang of the Bengay his grandmother rubbed on her bad back.

The smells were so vivid, so relaxing, so transporting that Mo'Steel wondered if he was losing his mind — and decided he didn't care. Baking bread. He'd forgotten anything could smell so delicious.

Then came the sounds. The soft slap, slap of dough being kneaded and turned, kneaded and turned. Latin jazz playing softly on a slightly tinny radio. And humming — his grandmother's robust humming.

"Storm's gaining — on us," Jobs hollered.

Dreamily, Mo'Steel played with the tiny Meanie

buttons under his fingers. The storm was bad. The winds looked strong enough to bring them down, make them crash. Some small part of his brain concentrated on trying to coax a little more speed out of his suit — but the best part of him was smelling that yeasty freshly baked bread smell and listening to his grandmother hum.

And then Mo'Steel wasn't just smelling and hearing his grandmother, he was *seeing* her.

The details were overwhelming. Details about her he'd forgotten without noticing. She was wearing those fleece sweatpants she loved, and her hair was tied back in a flowered scarf. Her shoulders were slightly hunched as she leaned over the counter, working the dough. She looked exactly as she had when Mo'Steel had been five or six years old and had spent long afternoons playing with his toy cars on her dusty kitchen floor, listening to her stories and superstitions.

They'd left her behind to board the *Mayflower*. She'd been too old to meet NASA's age requirement.

"Grandma?" Mo'Steel whispered, soothed by the familiar salt-and-pepper ponytail. "What are you making?"

Mo'Steel's grandmother turned to smile at him,

and his stomach went icy. She was crying — crying silent tears. The teardrops fell into the dough, and now Mo'Steel could see it glistening with her tears.

"You left me," his grandmother said, her red-rimmed eyes hard with anger.

Mo'Steel lost a minute to black terror. His mind shut down and when it blinked back on, his grandmother was gone.

The storm was closing in. Mo'Steel couldn't see much in the dim light. It took him a beat to realize he was falling. Headfirst. The frozen ash was rushing up. He could feel the cold radiating up off old Mother Earth.

"Mo'Steel! Mo, pull out of it! Pull out!"

Jobs. Jobs yelling.

With numb fingers, Mo'Steel gave his full attention to fumbling with the tiny Meanie buttons. He found the one that sent him flying up into the air. Pushed it.

Now the ground was rushing up twice as fast.

He was going to crash.

Forty yards.

Twenty.

Ten.

*   *   *

Edward shielded his eyes and looked at the sky. It lit up with a brilliant flash. After a pause came a rumbling crash that made him shiver.

That flashing light — it had a name, but Edward couldn't remember what it was. He remembered crawling into his mommy and daddy's bed, and Daddy saying nothing was wrong, the flashing light couldn't hurt him. . . .

But — but something *was* wrong now. Edward wanted to get away from the light and away from the wind that was blowing ash into his eyes. He'd waited and waited for the others to suggest they find shelter.

But they hadn't.

Olga was nearby, sitting under the brick chimney with her knees pulled up to her chest. Her eyes were closed and she kept moaning and kicking her feet. Edward thought maybe she was having a nightmare.

He wanted to ask Noyze if it was okay to wake Olga up. But Noyze was staring off into space and rocking back and forth, back and forth. Edward had tried to talk to her, but she didn't seem to hear him. . . .

Maybe he should go find the others. He thought D-Caf and Violet and Roger Dodger were together over by that lump of overpass, but getting to them meant walking by 2Face and 2Face was scaring Edward. She was walking in circles, shouting bad words at people who weren't there.

Could 2Face see ghosts?

Edward looked away from 2Face and his eyes fell on Billy. Billy was huddled up near Noyze. His shoulders slumped forward and his eyes were on the ashy ground.

Billy was weird. He knew things. Stuff about the future and stuff about other people. Sometimes Edward thought Billy even knew what he was *thinking*.

Edward didn't like to get close to Billy. But, but — well, he knew Jobs trusted Billy. If Jobs trusted him, he must be okay. Besides, there was nobody else . . .

Cautiously, Edward approached Billy's motionless form. He kneeled down and shook his shoulder. "Billy? Billy, I think — I think we should find shelter. It's raining."

Billy's head snapped up, sending Edward scrambling back. His mouth twisted into a cruel smile.

"What's the matter?" Billy said in a singsong voice. "Scared of a wittle wain? Didn't Mommy pack your umbrella?"

It wasn't Billy's voice.

Edward shuddered.

It was . . . the voice of Jackson Cooder. Edward's eyes widened in horror as Billy's pale face slowly changed until Edward found himself staring into the ratlike brown eyes that had taunted him during recess and P.E.

Jackson's eyes.

Five yards.

The ground was closing in fast.

Just before he might have crashed, Mo'Steel kicked his legs. Kicked hard enough to bring his head upright. His left foot grazed the frozen ground and his suit shot off at a strange angle. Another kick straightened him out and Mo'Steel shot into the air with a shout of triumph.

Jobs was about ten yards away, just head of him and slightly off to his right. "Mo, you okay?" he shouted uncertainly.

Mo'Steel laughed. "Yeah, I'm fine!"

"Un-believable," Jobs croaked.

"Yeah! Yeah, I'm invincible," Mo'Steel said, thinking of what he'd told Noyze. Suddenly, he was desperate to see her. To see Olga. They'd been gone for almost twenty hours. Anything could have happened in that much time.

"Let's go!" Mo'Steel called.

Jobs gave a weak nod and they resumed their previous course.

Mo'Steel's elation quickly faded. The gloom from the approaching storm was oppressive. The yellowish clouds were closer now, the lightning more frequent. The wind caught the ash and blew it into swirling eddies. Vivid images from his — What had that been? A nightmare? — came back to him. The only good thing was that the biting cold was softening.

"I — see them!" Jobs hollered.

Mo'Steel could see the others, too. 2Face was the only one up on her feet. The others were huddled down against the wind and swirling ash.

Only Edward looked up as Mo'Steel landed with a bump and immediately began struggling out of his clammy, ill-fitting suit. Edward stumbled to his feet, half running and half crawling toward them.

"Edward, what's wrong?" Mo'Steel demanded.

Edward looked fearfully over his shoulder. "Jack! Jack — was teasing me."

Mo'Steel just stared.

Now Jobs had brought his suit in for a careful landing. Edward threw himself at his brother's legs, hiding behind him, peeking out fearfully.

"Ed? Hey — what's going on?" Jobs asked, twisting around and trying to see his brother's face.

"Jack," Edward moaned. "Please — please don't let him —"

Jobs put an arm around Edward. "Don't — be silly," he croaked. "Nobody's going to hurt you."

Mo'Steel looked at Edward's frightened face and felt a burst of fear in his own chest.

Edward is right, a voice in his head whispered. They had to get away. His grandmother — and now Jack. An image of Jack floated into his mind. He was a vicious little kid.

Mo'Steel scanned the area carefully. Where was Jack hiding? He could be anywhere. . . .

There is no Jack, said another, calmer voice in the back of Mo'Steel's head. *And your grandmother has been gone for centuries.*

There! A flash of movement just behind him . . . Was it Jack? Mo'Steel spun around, eyes wide in the half-light.

There is no Jack. You're dreaming. . . .

I've got to get something to fight with, Mo'Steel thought. *I want to have a weapon when Jack attacks. . . .*

"There is no Jack!" Mo'Steel burst out. "I — we've got to get out of this storm."

Edward met his gaze and seemed to gain strength. "I know a place we can go. I saw some people go underground."

"Are — are you sure they were — real?" Jobs asked.

"I — yes," Edward said.

"Let's get the others," Jobs said.

"Mom!" Mo'Steel yelled, running against the howling wind toward the huddled figures of Olga, Noyze, and Billy. "Noyze! Come on!"

Noyze lifted her head and stared at Mo'Steel with haunted eyes. "We've got to find the *Mayflower*," she whispered hoarsely. "My father — he's still in his berth. I left him. . . ."

Mo'Steel put his hand under Noyze's arm and hauled her to her feet. "It's the storm," he murmured. "We'll all feel better once we get out of this storm."

CHAPTER THIRTEEN

OFF, OFF, OFF! ENOUGH!

Billy's mind was a database of memories that belonged to him and ones he'd stolen from the eighty people who'd traveled with him through space. Most of those people were dead but their dreams and fantasies lived on in Billy's mind, and now the strange storm swirling above his head twisted those memories into ugly flashes —

A dog struggling against the current in a storm-swollen stream —

Stop.

An ax glinting in firelight —

Stop.

A heart monitor beep, beep, beeping —

Stop.

A woman laughing bitterly —

Stop.

Billy felt a surge of panic as he realized how hard

he was concentrating to stop the images from developing — he had to concentrate to keep them from growing from harmless nothings into horror, into gore. As soon as he had one under control, another would ooze up to take its place.

Stop.

Stop.

Stop.

A minuscule part of Billy's brain moved his right foot forward, then his left, right, left. He was vaguely aware of himself trudging after the disorganized group as they followed Edward across the ashy plain, carefully picking their way around obstacles.

Billy had tried to visit Edward's thoughts, to find out if Edward truly believed he'd seen people disappearing into an underground shelter.

But Edward's thoughts were a jumble.

And Billy couldn't spare much time. The visions were crowding him, threatening to overwhelm him, to drive him crazy. Billy wanted to think about it, puzzle out the best way to survive, the best way for all of them to survive, but, but . . .

His brain buzzed with nightmare images. He was trying to hit the OFF button on a thousand different horror movies with one remote.

Off.

Bullies taunting Edward, playing keep-away with his link, tossing it in circles around the tetherball pole, leering at his attempts to lunge for it —

Off.

D-Caf ordering a Big Mac and receiving hundreds of pea-green worms in a cardboard box —

Off.

Nightmares in English, in Spanish, in Chinese, in languages he didn't understand. Familiar faces, strange faces — beautiful, ugly, hated, loved.

Violet's mother going over the edge of the U.S.S. *Constitution* —

A Rider boomerang flying toward Roger Dodger —

Off, off, off! Enough!

Billy summoned up all of his will and slammed the door on the flood of images.

Silence.

For a moment, Billy could hear nothing but the synapses of his own brain firing, firing, firing. It was like catching your breath after fleeing from a madman.

Peace.

Quiet.

At one time, Billy had feared being alone in his own mind. His consciousness had absorbed five hundred years of void on the *Mayflower* and he'd thought nothing could be worse than being alone.

Now he welcomed the quiet.

The stillness of his own mind.

But then — then . . .

Billy's brain revved up like a motor set on autopilot, rushing to fill the void, accessing random memories, spinning fantasies, creating new nightmare images. . . .

He was back on the *Mayflower,* locked in his berth with nothing to see but the unchanging tableau of the hibernation berth's lid, the wire mesh catwalk above it, the shadow of the berths stacked above his.

He stood in his crib, wailing for attention from the fleeting dark shapes passing by, banging the railings with tiny numb fingers.

He was in his sweet warm bed in Texas when he felt the furtive movement of a snake under the sheets —

He tried to shut it down, to bring back the peace, but his concentration, his control failed him. The deluge of images crowded in, too vast, too gruesome to resist.

Billy pressed his hands to his head, whimpering.

He couldn't stop the images and he couldn't live with them. . . .

Whispers —

A soft thud —

There was only one thing to do.

Billy reached down inside himself, felt the relentless fluttering of his heart, and held on.

Violet stared at the concrete wall. It looked so solid, so real. She was reaching out to touch it when time stopped.

Time passed. How much time Violet didn't know. It was like she'd been suddenly frozen.

The wall swam back into Violet's vision. Concrete, a concrete wall with evenly spaced circular holes. It looked real. Benign. Violet reached out one trembling hand to touch it. The surface felt cool and rough under her fingers, exactly the way she remembered concrete feeling. She turned her hand and studied the thin coating of dust on her palm, expecting some trick, expecting her hand to melt or to break out into welts or —

But no. Nothing happened. There was just the dust, nothing more.

Violet immediately turned and rested her back against the wall. She could hear a stealthy movement, feel something scurrying around her ankles, but she couldn't see what it was. The only light was coming from a circular opening way above her head, like a sewer with the grate removed. She couldn't remember getting here . . . the last thing she remembered was Jobs and Mo'Steel coming back and saying they had to find shelter, Edward knew where they could go. . . .

"Where am I?" she whispered, her voice sounding dry and husky.

"I don't know," came D-Caf's voice. He sounded — okay. Real. "It's dark," he added.

"Find your flashlight," Violet whispered, groping for her own and surprised to find it hanging around her waist, exactly where she'd left it before the nightmares had begun.

"We're in the bunker," Edward rasped out. "I told you I saw — I knew about this place."

A little cry of relief escaped Violet's lips. She wanted badly to believe the strange visions were gone, so she ignored the powerful feeling of being watched, and the sick-cat smell that had suddenly surrounded them. "The storm," she said. "I think —"

"Atmospheric," Jobs muttered. "Psychotropic."

"The storm," Olga said, sounding shaken.

"I think we're safe —" Violet was still fumbling

with her flashlight when a blaze of light blinded her. She shielded her eyes with one hand, squinting in the brilliant light.

Now she could see Mo'Steel, Jobs, 2Face, Edward squinting in the light and she watched as terror dawned on their faces. In a circle behind them were another row of faces. Impossible faces. Human faces crisscrossed with shiny scar tissue, mouths with pointy gray teeth, bodies covered with scrappy fur vests, matted hair twisted around tiny glittering rodent fangs. Yellow eyes gleaming with intelligence and malice.

"Monsters," Roger Dodger whispered.

The monster closest to Violet reached out a filthy hand and grabbed her face. "Get out," he snarled.

Violet's knees quivered.

The nightmares had just begun.

CHAPTER FOURTEEN

IT'S A DREAM . . .

A glint caught Mo'Steel's eye and he realized the monster closest to him had drawn a crude knife, like a rusty lid off a can of tuna fish bent into shape.

"They've got weapons!" Mo'Steel yelled, but by then the torch-lit corridor was echoing with confusion and noise.

Mo'Steel saw Violet fending off what looked like a very strange-looking girl and D-Caf, sounding panicked, was shouting at her, "Should I go worm? Should I?" Jobs was ordering Edward to hide — which was a joke since the kid was practically invisible even if you knew he was there. Noyze and Olga were huddled against the wall, hiding Roger Dodger between them.

It's a dream, Mo'Steel told himself. *Visions.*

But he had only a second to think that, because the monster closest to him, the bald one with the tin-can knife, launched himself at Mo'Steel with a snarl and knocked him onto his back.

Mo'Steel gasped for breath. Baldy scrambled on top of him and pressed a very heavy knee into his rib cage.

Mo'Steel felt the knife edge pressing into his jugular vein. He breathed in Baldy's rank breath and fumbled for the boomerang hooked in his belt. So what if Baldy was a vision? That didn't mean Mo'-Steel couldn't kick his butt.

But — but when Mo'Steel looked again, the ugly, scarred bald guy was gone — he had been replaced by the equally scary face of Sister Francesca, the nun who'd taught him in Sunday school. She was wearing her brown habit and giving him a familiar scowl.

"Are j'ou Savagers?"

"Wh — what?" Mo'Steel sputtered.

Sister Francesca had transformed back into Baldy.

"I will ask you to please remove yourself from my classroom until such time as you can act like a young gentleman." Baldy's mouth moved and Sister Francesca's clipped tones came out.

"No," Mo'Steel grunted. "That storm is crazy. I don't want to go outside."

He had the boomerang out now. The blade wasn't as sharp as it once was, but Mo'Steel whipped it around fast and rammed it into Baldy's back.

Baldy yelped with pain and surprise. Then he was rolling away, grasping frantically at the blade and cursing loudly.

Mo'Steel struggled up onto his knees, watching Baldy stagger around. For a moment Mo'Steel felt terrible for thinking it, but he knew he needed the boomerang back. It was the only weapon he had.

Mo'Steel hauled himself to his feet. He'd never felt so crappy. He was dizzy, gasping for breath, confused. Was this a dream — or what? The pain in his ribs felt real enough. Okay, so it was real. But then why could he hear organ music? Handel's Hallelujah Chorus.

With a desperate effort, Baldy pulled the blade free with his beefy hand. He turned to Mo'Steel with a leering smile, brandishing the weapon. "Lookin' for this?"

Before Mo'Steel could come up with a smart reply, Baldy grabbed his arms, pulled them roughly together behind Mo'Steel's back, and pressed the boomerang to his neck. "J'ou Savagers?" he demanded stubbornly.

"I don't — no!"

"Then where j'ou steal water?"

"I didn't steal any water!"

"J'ou are fat with it, j'ou dirty . . ."

The blade was pressing into Mo'Steel's neck. Now was not the time to go into a long story about Mother and Yago and the Troika. . . .

A grunt over on Mo'Steel's right. The torch fell, someone — it sounded like D-Caf — screamed and they were plunged into total darkness. Baldy loosened his grip on Mo'Steel's arms for a split second —

Long enough. Mo'Steel threw all of his weight to his left and Baldy lost his grip. Blindly, Mo'Steel swung a fist — felt it connect solidly. Swung again — missed. Took his weight on his left leg and kicked out with his right.

"Ouch!" Sister Francesca's voice — and the clatter of the boomerang on the concrete floor.

Mo'Steel dropped to his knees, feeling frantically for the blade, completely unable to see a thing in the inky blackness.

Baldy was close. Mo'Steel could smell his breath. Desperately, Mo'Steel swept both arms with wide arcs. He knocked up against the boomerang and felt it slice into his fingertips. Ignoring the pain, he grabbed it.

Baldy lunged at Mo'Steel in the dark. One arm

caught Mo'Steel around the shoulder. Baldy grabbed Mo'Steel's upper arm tightly and yanked it hard. Mo'Steel felt a strange, intense sensation on his leg, and a second later the hot wave of pain hit him. Baldy still had his tin-can knife. And for a tin can it cut pretty good.

This was bad. Mo'Steel didn't want to die. His mom might need him. Or Jobs. Or Noyze. He could still hear the sounds of fighting, but he couldn't tell if the others were in big trouble.

The pain was getting harder to ignore. His leg was throbbing with every beat of his heart. Baldy hooked a leg under Mo'Steel and tried to pull his legs out from under him.

Mo'Steel slashed out blindly — jabbing the boomerang up, down, left, right, until he felt the blade connect. He pulled it free and jabbed again.

Mo'Steel sat down, breathing hard. He pushed himself backward with his feet until he was pressed up against the wall. A strange roaring filled his ears, but he thought he heard Noyze sobbing.

"Noyze?" Mo'Steel fumbled for his flashlight with his left hand. His right hand was a stiff glove — swollen from small boomerang cuts. Numb. He got the light on and swung it over the ground.

There was Baldy.

He was lying on his back at Mo'Steel's feet. Motionless.

"Hawk!" someone screamed.

Footsteps. And then a couple of the monster people ran into Mo'Steel's flashlight beam. They knelt next to Baldy.

Two scary scarred faces stared at Mo'Steel with wonder.

Suddenly, Mo'Steel's head felt very heavy. He decided to look for Noyze and finish talking to the monster people in a minute. He let his head rest on his knees, closed his eyes, and drifted off.

CHAPTER FIFTEEN

"FOOD."

Jobs opened his eyes. Directly in front of him was a table. An ordinary blue metal table with a stainless steel top — the kind you might see in a doctor's office. On top of the table was a grubby glass containing a half inch of water.

Water . . .

Jobs sat up with a jerk, grabbed the glass with shaky hands, and poured the water into his trembling mouth. His fuzzy tongue immediately absorbed most of the water. A tiny trickle reached his throat, releasing a taste like rotten cottage cheese. He was suddenly aware of a thick, gritty substance coating his teeth.

More, he thought, greedily looking around.

The room was almost completely empty. There was the small bed he was sitting on and one other. D-Caf was sleeping there with a rough brown blanket half-covering him. Next to him was another blue metal table and another dirty glass. Apparently, D-Caf hadn't woken up yet because his glass still contained a half inch of water.

Jobs licked his lips and eased himself up to kneeling. His blanket fell away and he suddenly realized most of his clothes were gone.

D-Caf stretched, rolled over, and opened his eyes.

Jobs jerked back under his blanket and tried to remember how he got there.

D-Caf sat up quickly. "Where are we? Hey! Where are my clothes?"

"No idea," Jobs said, thinking of Edward and Violet and Mo'Steel. "And the others — what happened to them?"

"I remember — we were in some sort of hallway," D-Caf said dreamily, narrowing his eyes. "And then we were attacked by the Pittsburgh Steelers — they were really ticked — wait, maybe that was a dream. . . ."

"Yeah, maybe." Jobs smiled at D-Caf's confusion. "I was having some pretty weird dreams myself."

"Violet and I talked about it a little," D-Caf said. "You know, while you were gone. She thought maybe the storm —"

"Shh — listen!"

D-Caf obediently fell silent. The two boys sat listening tensely. Jobs stared hard at the concrete block wall behind his bed. And then the sound came again.

A furtive sound — a gerbil with a paper-towel roll. Chewing, the scrambling of tiny, clawed feet . . .

"Hear that?" Jobs whispered.

D-Caf nodded, wide-eyed. "Sounds like — rats."

Jobs's eyes swept the room, but it was still practically empty: two beds, two blankets, two tables, two glasses.

A cell.

Where *were* they?

Moving swiftly, Jobs got off his bed, wrapped his blanket around his waist, and approached the door. It had a metal frame painted the same blue as the tables. The long, narrow pane of glass was crisscrossed with metal fibers in a diamond pattern. Jobs tried the stainless handle. Locked.

He pressed his nose to the glass. Outside was a bare hallway with a concrete floor. Several doors much like the one he was pressing his body against opened off of it. A girl was coming down the hallway — a girl Jobs had never seen before. *Not* a Remnant!

Jobs goggled. Where had she come from?

This — his mind had a difficult time forming the thought — this meant that other people had survived the Rock. Edward was right! Jobs was so shocked that he let the blanket drop.

Questions swirled in his mind. *How* had she survived? Were there others? How many . . . ?

"D-Caf," Jobs croaked. "There's a girl out there. . . ."

D-Caf leaped out of bed and pressed close to Jobs's shoulder, angling for a position at the window. "One of *our* girls, you mean?"

"No," Jobs said wonderingly. "Someone else. Do you know what this means?"

D-Caf gave a little yelp and jumped away from the window. "She's coming this way!"

Jobs's first reaction was delight. He had so many questions he wanted to ask. . . . Then he realized he was standing there with a blanket around his ankles. He was eager to make new friends, but he wanted his clothes back first.

As the strange girl stepped close to the door and withdrew a key, he snatched up the coarse blanket, hopped back onto the bed, and covered himself up.

The door swung open, and there she was — a short and slight girl who was watching them warily.

She had Asian features, Jobs thought. Brown almond-shaped eyes and olive skin. But her hair was light brown, not black. She wore a crude pair of wide-legged pants and a tunic made of the same material as the blanket Jobs was clutching in both hands.

"Food," she said slowly. Keeping her eyes pinned suspiciously on D-Caf, she awkwardly held out two small bowls to Jobs.

Jobs took one bowl in each hand. Inside was what looked like a tiny bundle of twiggy herbs. Jobs held one bowl out to D-Caf who took it curiously. He put the other bowl in his lap.

The girl had already edged back toward the door — her hand was grasping the doorknob — he wanted to say something to make her stay. "Jobs," he said, pointing to himself.

She looked nervously at D-Caf. Then, giving Jobs a fleeting, worried smile, she placed a delicate hand on her own chest. "Echo."

Excitement exploded in Jobs's chest.

There was still life on Earth!

Jobs had thought he'd led the Remnants into a

tomb, but seeing this girl changed everything. He hadn't been wrong to think Earth could still sustain life. The Remnants weren't alone. There were *people* here. That meant they had a source of water, a supply of food. He hadn't been a total idiot talking the others into coming back!

A huge weight he didn't even know he was carrying lifted off Jobs. No matter what happened now, it wasn't all his fault. He hadn't been a total jerk. . . .

"Where are we?" D-Caf asked.

The girl — Echo — trembled. She eased closer to the door, casting a frightened look at D-Caf.

"Don't worry," Jobs said hastily. "We won't hurt you."

Echo kept her hand on the doorknob, poised to flee. She seemed to trust Jobs, fearing only D-Caf.

"J'ou are underground," she told Jobs hesitantly, as if she couldn't expect him to understand her language. She did have a heavy accent, vaguely Russian-sounding, but Jobs understood her quite clearly.

"I — I know that," Jobs said slowly. "But what is this place? How did it survive the Rock? How old are you? Are you alone here?"

"Why are we locked in?" D-Caf added.

The girl flinched at the sound of D-Caf's voice.

"Hang on, D-Caf," Jobs said quietly. "Can't you see she's afraid of you?"

"She doesn't even know me," D-Caf said resentfully.

"Just be quiet!" Jobs said. "He won't hurt you," he added soothingly, addressing the girl. "Can't you — j'ou — tell us something more about this place?"

"This is the Alphas' home," the girl said, still speaking slowly. "A biosphere."

Jobs sat up excitedly. "Built before the Rock hit, right?"

Echo nodded slowly. "I'm twenty-fifth generation here," the girl said. "Long ago, there was an asteroid —"

"Right!" Jobs exclaimed. "Somehow . . . somehow, I bet some scientists learned about the Rock before it hit. Learned long enough before to build this place and keep it secret —"

"J'ou are right," Echo said. "And j'ou. Have j'ou come from away, from the sky?"

"No," Jobs said. "We are Earthlings!"

D-Caf snorted. "Earthlings? Jobs, this isn't a bad space movie."

"I mean, Americans," Jobs said in confusion. "Humans. We were born on this planet, but —"

"Where are our friends?" D-Caf demanded harshly. "Are our friends here?"

"Seven friends," Echo said. "Safe like j'ou."

"Prisoners?" D-Caf said.

"Only seven?" Jobs said. "That means we lost someone. . . ."

Jobs thought suddenly of Edward. Was he here? Jobs last remembered seeing him in the hallway. . . .

"Is there a little boy here?" he asked Echo urgently. "A six-year-old boy?"

"He is here," Echo said, and again her expression was guarded. "Is he your son?"

"My son?" Jobs repeated. "No, no . . . he's my brother."

"What is a — brother?" Echo asked.

"We — we have the same mother and father," Jobs explained.

Echo smiled, and shook her head in amusement. "I must go now."

"Wait!" Jobs said. "What — what are you going to do with us? Can't you let us out of here? Can't you let me see my brother?"

"I can't, I'm not allowed," Echo said solemnly.

"The Alphas are prisoners, too. We are waiting for the Marauders to decide."

"The Marauders?" Jobs repeated. "Who —"

But Echo was shaking her head. She slipped through the door, leaving Jobs with lots of unanswered questions.

CHAPTER SIXTEEN

"I WANT TO SEE MY FRIENDS."

Someone was watching him.

Mo'Steel knew it in the seconds after he woke up, even before he opened his eyes. Pretending to be asleep, he felt for his boomerang. It was tucked under his belt, just like it was supposed to be. He opened his eyes cautiously — and quickly sat up in alarm, drawing his weapon.

He was inside — in some sort of small, smelly room with people all around him. They wore crude garments of stitched-together skins and their hair was matted and dirty.

Mo'Steel quickly scanned their faces. They were strangers. But — but how was that possible? And why were they watching him so suspiciously? Was this another dream?

"Where — where am I?" Mo'Steel asked, struggling to sit up. As soon as he moved, a hot pain shot through his leg. Mo'Steel let a moan escape. He was usually good with pain, but this was different — he felt feverish.

A dark-skinned woman scurried up to him. "Sit, sit," she said nervously.

Mo'Steel eased himself down. "Who are you?" he asked suspiciously, still thinking this had to be a dream. The Remnants were the only survivors of the Rock — weren't they?

"I am Aga."

She was old — older even than Mo'Steel's mother. He could see a few strands of gray in her dark hair. She had puffy circles under her eyes and her fingernails were torn and dirty. She sounded exhausted as she handed Mo'Steel a strange bladderlike container and said, "Drink."

Mo'Steel didn't want whatever she was offering him, but he was worried someone might stab him if he refused. Four young, powerful-looking armed men were eyeing him with open hostility. So Mo'-Steel accepted the container and took the tiniest possible sip.

Water. Tasted stale, but okay.

He relaxed and gulped down some more, realizing just how thirsty he was. The water was stale — but delicious. He was tipping the bladder back for a third time when the woman, Aga, jerked it from his hands.

"That's enough!" she said, sounding horrified. She tested the weight of the bladder and studied him angrily. "J'ou didn't have to drink it *all*."

"I — I'm sorry," Mo'Steel muttered. Obviously, he'd been incredibly rude. He cast a nervous glance at the four young men. They were bunched together, whispering. About him, no doubt.

Aga quickly recovered her composure. "No — no, I'm the one who is sorry," she said meekly. "Anything I have is j'ours to take."

Mo'Steel was baffled. Why was Aga giving him water? Wasn't he a prisoner? And for that matter, why hadn't these people killed him? Or at least taken his weapon away from him?

"Where am I?" Mo'Steel asked.

"Alpha bunker," Aga said uneasily. She seemed as if she wanted to escape but didn't dare. Mo'Steel noticed that the others were drawing closer, trying to hear without being too obvious about it. That made him even more nervous.

"So — so you are an Alpha?" Mo'Steel asked hesitantly.

The woman looked decidedly insulted. "We are Marauders!"

"Oh." Now Mo'Steel was even more confused. He wished Jobs was with him. Or Violet. Or Noyze. Someone who would know what to ask. Where were the others?

"My friends?" he asked uncertainly, not sure he wanted to hear the answer.

"Locked up."

"But — but why am I here?" Mo'Steel asked.

"J'ou do not remember?" Aga asked suspiciously.

"Remember what?" Mo'Steel asked hesitantly. An angry murmur went through the group and Mo'Steel thought he heard someone say, "If he doesn't even *remember* —" But the others quickly shushed whoever had spoken.

An elderly man stepped toward Mo'Steel and now it was obvious that the entire room full of people was listening closely. "Tell us exactly what j'ou *do* remember," the man said.

There was an uneasy pause, and Mo'Steel suddenly got a flash of a fight in a dimly lit corridor. He'd been fighting a half man, half nun. But that had been a dream . . . or had it? Mo'Steel's hands were cut from the boomerang.

"I remember a fight," Mo'Steel said slowly. "I — I think I really injured a man, a big, bald man. . . ."

To Mo'Steel's great surprise, this seemed to cut the tension. Aga actually smiled. "That's right," she said encouragingly. "J'ou destroyed Hawk. He was our leader and now that he's dead, j'ou're our new leader —"

"*Will* be," the elderly man said. "If he survives the Beasts. . . ."

Mo'Steel's shock must have shown on his face because Aga leaned closer and whispered, "Don't worry. We can't travel until the dream storm has passed. Your hands will have some time to heal."

"Th-thanks," Mo'Steel mumbled. He was having a hard time accepting this bit of luck. *He* was the Marauders' new leader? That was hard to believe. What a strange way of dealing with someone who kills your leader. . . .

But then Aga withdrew and Mo'Steel saw the four young men watching him. Uh-oh. He would bet these guys wanted him dead.

Four against one.

Bad odds.

"Aga!" Mo'Steel tried to sound commanding but his voice came out squeaky.

She turned slowly. "Yes?"

"I want to see my friends," Mo'Steel said, wondering if the Marauders would actually do what he said.

"All of them?" Aga asked blandly.

Mo'Steel considered. In a way he wanted to see everyone, to make sure they were okay. But then again, he had some major decisions to make and he didn't need 2Face arguing and D-Caf making stupid jokes.

"Just three," he told Aga. "I want you to bring them to me immediately. And we'll need a private place to talk."

Aga hesitated for the briefest moment, and then nodded. "Give me their names and we will bring them."

CHAPTER SEVENTEEN

Aga led Mo'Steel into a dusty room not much bigger than a closet and left without a word. Mo'Steel noticed she didn't lock the door.

He could escape. . . .

But where would he go? Back out into the dream storm? Mo'Steel shuddered. No. No, he definitely didn't want to do that. . . .

He stood awkwardly on his good leg, holding the hurt one slightly off the ground, waiting for the others to arrive, worrying they wouldn't. What if this was all a trap?

But then Jobs appeared in the doorway. He was accompanied by a girl Mo'Steel hadn't seen before. Compared to the Marauders, she looked clean and civilized. *An Alpha,* Mo'Steel told himself.

Jobs spotted Mo'Steel and a look of immense relief crossed his face. The girl disappeared down the hallway as Jobs stepped into the little room.

"Mo!" Jobs exclaimed, looking like he was about to hug Mo'Steel.

"Hi, Duck," Mo'Steel said and gave his buddy a quick hug and a slap on the back.

"You — you look awful," Jobs said.

"Gee, Duck, you don't look so great yourself. Geez."

"No, Mo, seriously," Jobs persisted. "Are you okay? That storm was pretty — strange. And I think we were attacked in that hallway. Everything is so muddled. . . ."

"I think my leg's infected," Mo'Steel said casually.

"Have you seen Violet or Edward?" Jobs asked urgently. "D-Caf is okay. He's in the room with me. They took our clothes. Then they suddenly brought mine back and told me to come in here. I couldn't get any explanation. Do you know what's —"

Jobs trailed off as Noyze and Olga came into the room together. They both looked tired and worried, Mo'Steel thought. Noyze had a big scabby scratch across her nose.

Olga immediately pulled Mo'Steel into a tight hug. "Oh, honey, I'm so glad you're okay," she said, smoothing down his hair.

"Ow, Mom, I can't breathe —"

Olga let him go and went to hug Jobs.

Noyze was standing a few steps away, smiling at Mo'Steel shyly. Her eyes were bright with tears. Mo'Steel slipped his tough-looking sliced-and-diced hand into hers and flinched when she squeezed.

"Listen, we got a big problem," he said to cover the awkward moment. As quickly as possible, he explained about Hawk and the Marauders and how he was apparently their leader now.

"*If* — and I quote — *if* I survive the Beasts," Mo'Steel said.

"Who or what are the Beasts?" Olga asked, her face creased with worry.

"Dunno," Mo'Steel admitted. "I — I felt stupid asking."

Jobs had gone very pale. "You've got to say no," he said urgently. "I — I have a bad feeling about this. Just tell the Marauders thanks, but no thanks."

Mo'Steel trusted Jobs's opinion — but bunny out? He didn't like the sound of that.

Olga was shaking her head. "Not so fast," she said uneasily. "We don't know how the Marauders will react if Mo'Steel refuses their little test."

"Some of them seem ready to get rid of me

now," Mo'Steel admitted, thinking of the four guys who'd watched him so suspiciously.

"You're the leader because you defeated their leader," Noyze said nervously. "That means anyone who gets to you —"

"Yeah," Mo'Steel said. "I thought of that."

"Why don't we just get out of here?" Jobs said, full of edgy energy. "Mo'Steel can order the Marauders to let everyone out of their rooms, and then we can just take off."

"And go where?" Olga asked quietly.

"I — I don't know," Jobs admitted. "We didn't find any water in the Dark Zone, but now we know there must be some somewhere. Maybe we can — I don't know. I need some time to think."

"This is the Alphas' bunker," Olga said thoughtfully. "But the Alphas seem scared of the Marauders. Mo asked them to let us out of our cells, and the Alphas obeyed."

Jobs nodded quickly. "I spoke to this Alpha girl. Her name is Echo, and she said the Alphas were the Marauders' prisoners, too."

"So if Mo'Steel became the Marauders' leader, he could order the Alphas to do whatever he wanted with the bunker," Olga said.

"What do you have in mind?" Noyze asked.

"Resting," Olga said with a profound sigh.

"Here?" Mo'Steel demanded.

Olga nodded wearily. "Granted, it ain't Miami Beach. It's old and uh, fragrant, but think about it. This place is as safe as any we've seen since the Rock hit. It sure beats Mother."

"You want to stay *here*?" Mo'Steel couldn't quite keep the distaste out of his voice.

"Don't worry," Olga said with a laugh. "I'm not saying *you* should stay. But — well, I think this is as close as we're going to get to 'happily ever after.' I'd stay here. And I think it would be a good place for Roger Dodger and Edward."

"I understand what you're saying," Jobs interrupted. He turned and gave Mo'Steel a pleading look. "It's just — I have a bad feeling about these Beasts. I really don't think we should —"

"Sorry, Duck, it's no use," Mo'Steel said. "If Mom wants me to fight the Beasts — end of discussion."

Jobs wished he could go back to his little cell and think things through. But that wasn't happening.

"We'd better not leave the Marauders alone for too long," Mo'Steel said. "They could be planning to ambush us right now. You guys come back to their room with me. I'll send Aga for the others."

"Hmm," Olga said as they ventured cautiously out of the little room and followed Mo'Steel down the hallway. "You're enjoying this, aren't you? You already sound comfortable giving orders."

Noyze smiled shakily. "Yeah, what are we supposed to call you now? King Mo'Steel?"

"*Mon* Steel" Olga suggested.

"Mo'Majesty!" Noyze said, smiling.

"Your Greatness will do," Mo'Steel said grandly. He indicated a door. "In here."

The Marauders stared as the four of them filed into the room. Jobs stared, too. These — people — were nothing like Echo. He'd once visited a museum in North Dakota and the Marauders reminded him of early photographs of the Plains Indians, taken before the Europeans wiped them out. They were savage, wild-looking, noble, and completely foreign.

Jobs felt weak in the knees. Mo'Steel was supposed to be in charge of these people?

"Aga!" Mo'Steel said, and a hunched old woman who was missing an ear scuttled forward. "Please get the rest of our friends and bring them here."

Aga looked pinched and disapproving, but she moved off — apparently to do what Mo'Steel said.

Meanwhile, Noyze and Olga began to do something Jobs would never have considered — they were moving through the crowd of Marauders, introducing themselves.

Jobs stuck close to Mo'Steel. "Mo, I have a weird feeling that girl over there knocked me silly," he said uneasily. "I remember her from my dream or whatever it was —"

"Should I order her to kiss your feet or something?"

"No, no, that's okay," Jobs said, not laughing.

Noyze came back, and Mo'Steel led her off to a corner for a private talk. Jobs felt nervous and exposed. What if the Marauders attacked him? He was alone and unarmed. Then Edward came in and hurried over to him.

"You okay?" Jobs demanded.

Edward nodded eagerly. "I *told* you I saw people!" he said excitedly. "They survived the Rock, too! Isn't that neat?"

"Yeah," Jobs admitted. His eyes were on the door, waiting to see what kind of shape the others were in.

Roger Dodger greeted them all matter-of-factly. A Marauder boy who looked about Roger Dodger's age was watching him curiously from across the room. Olga took Roger Dodger by the hand and introduced them.

Violet and 2Face came in together. Violet was pale, but composed. She met Jobs's gaze briefly and then looked quickly away. Jobs wanted to talk to her, but then D-Caf arrived and hurried over to her and Jobs changed his mind.

2Face stormed up to Jobs. She looked totally fine — no cuts or bruises. "*What* is going on?" she demanded angrily.

"Mo saved our skin," Jobs told her coldly.

"Oh, and how did he do that?"

"Got himself elected king," Jobs said.

"Ooooookay. Right," 2Face said shortly.

Jobs gave her a condensed version of the story, including the fact that Mo'Steel had to battle the Beasts to earn the right to lead the Marauders.

2Face didn't look at all pleased with the news. She narrowed her eyes and looked suspiciously around the room. "Where's Billy?"

Jobs was caught off guard. "I — I don't know." He saw that Aga had come back. Nervously, he approached the old woman; 2Face tagged along.

"Um, we're missing someone," he said hesitantly. "A guy. About my age —"

2Face pushed forward. "Pale, scrawny. Dark hair, dark eyes —"

Aga shrugged. "This is everyone." She indicated the people in the room and then began to turn away.

2Face grabbed Aga's shoulder and pulled her roughly back. "Tell me what you did with him!"

Jobs looked up and saw they were surrounded by angry Marauders. They had drawn crude weapons — rusty scraps of metal, sharpened sticks — and they looked ready to use them.

"2Face," Jobs said carefully, "stop."

"Sure." 2Face didn't move. "As soon as she tells me where Billy is."

Mo'Steel pushed into the circle. His face was flushed and his eyes looked too bright. Olga and Noyze were right behind him.

"2Face?" Mo'Steel asked. "What's going on?"

"You're making a fool of yourself, King Mo'Steel," 2Face said nastily.

"Oh? How's that?"

"Can't you see this is a trap?" 2Face shouted. "Don't you think it's a little funny that Billy disappeared so conveniently? He's in league with them! They're setting us up!"

There was a heavy pause.

Even the Marauders seemed to understand he was mocking 2Face. They looked at Mo'Steel for some sign. Mo'Steel smiled, Aga walked away from 2Face, the Marauders put their weapons away, the moment passed.

2Face stalked off into a corner.

Jobs turned to Mo'Steel, feeling shaken and tense. The other Remnants were also gathering around, looking worried.

"When was the last time you saw Billy?" Jobs asked, keeping his voice down so the Marauders wouldn't hear him.

"He left camp with us," Violet said certainly. "I remember being relieved he was keeping up. I was thinking about when we first landed in the shuttle and we had to carry him —"

"Did anyone see him in the corridor?" Jobs said quietly. "Before the Marauders attacked us?"

The others thought it over and then slowly shook their heads.

"Do you really think Billy would set us up?" D-Caf asked.

"Nah," Mo'Steel said.

"I think 2Face is a bigger problem," Jobs said honestly.

"She's not exactly an ambassador of peace," Noyze said unhappily. Her eyes traveled to the corner where 2Face was snarling at anyone who got too close.

"Enemies without, enemies within," Jobs said.

Mo'Steel clasped him on the back. "That's about the shape of things, Duck," he said. "Same story, different day."

K.A. APPLEGATE

REMNANTS™

Aftermath

FIRST I GOT TO DEAL WITH SOME BEASTS.

Mo'Steel was a mess. His fingers and hands had been cut up by the sharp edges of his stolen Rider boomerang. His thigh boasted a gouge the size and color of a raw Mickey D's hamburger — except for where it oozed yellow-green pus. Antibiotics? Not happening.

Face it, 'migo, Mo'Steel thought. *If this infection doesn't clear up soon, you're toast.*

The slash across the front of his neck was maddeningly itchy, a good sign according to his mom, a sign that the infection was healing. She'd stitched his thigh as best she could, using thread made from plant fibers and an actual sewing needle from the days before the Rock, given — secretly — by a woman named Marina. She'd slipped the sewing stuff to Mo'Steel's mom with a warning against joining her son on such a dangerous journey with the Marauders. Olga had thanked Marina and gotten busy with her stitching.

Mo'Steel's neck had decided to close up on its own. Good.

Mo'Steel was no stranger to stitches, but in this very disturbing bizarro Earth, it was clear that those who were healthiest ruled. The fewer serious injuries, the better.

So, the Marauders couldn't know about the ache in his ribs where Hawk had sat on him, crushing his chest. Nor could they know about the pain caused by the popped shoulder joint, also courtesy of the big, bald, and seriously ugly Hawk.

Mo'Steel refused to let the Marauders know what real damage Hawk had done to him.

Hawk.

The Marauders' former leader. Mo'Steel's predecessor.

Man, this is so not good, Mo'Steel thought, not for the first time since waking up flat on his back in the Alpha bunker, surrounded by a rag tag group of Marauders, barely able to remember who he was, let alone how he'd gotten there.

And now, the dream storm had finally passed and he was starting out on a journey through the Shadow Zone, into the Dark Zone, where a battle awaited him. A battle that would solidify his leadership or kill him.

Mo'Majesty. *Not yet,* he thought. *First I got to deal with some Beasts.*

"J'ou be careful," Echo said. She touched Jobs's arm lightly, briefly, and he felt the familiar blush flood his cheeks. This Alpha colony girl looked only a few years older than him, yet she had a wisdom about her that almost made her seem like an adult.

"Okay," Jobs said, taking a small step away from Echo and her serious brown eyes.

"There are many dangers out there. We have seen some from our observation station. And the Marauders tell us so."

"Okay," Jobs said again. "Uh, like what? Besides the flaming gas and all."

And, he added silently, *the awful, nagging scritching of little feet, always just out of sight . . .*

Echo didn't answer him.

"Can you tell us what else to steer clear of?" Jobs said, wondering if maybe he'd been unclear the first time.

Echo still remained silent. Instead, her eyes darted to the Marauders gathered at the back of the low-ceilinged room.

Jobs got it. The other, unspoken dangers lay with the Marauders themselves. Job had seen that they were unpredictable and brutal. So, if there was more to watch out for, he and the others would have to be on their guard at all times.

Which would, no doubt, be easier said than done.

Jobs felt very, very tired. The last thing he wanted to do was to go to the Dark Zone. But he had to. For Mo'Steel.

If it was the end of the world, what would you do?

Check out the official

REMNANTS™

Web site at

http://www.scholastic.com/remnants

and

- Tell the world what you would do if an asteroid was heading toward Earth.

- Play "The Escape" and discover if you have what it takes to secure a berth on the *Mayflower*.

- Find out information about the Remnants, including who is still alive.

Log on...while you still have a chance.